Misty and Me

Other APPLE PAPERBACKS you will want to read:

About the author

Barbara Girion lives in Short Hills, New Jersey, with her husband and three children. A former teacher, she has been active in theater work and has developed scripts and education programs for both adults and children. Most of her story ideas come from real life. Another of her books, *The Chicken Bone Wish*, is also available in an Apple Paperback edition from Scholastic, Inc.

Misty and Me

by
Barbara Girion

AN
APPLE
PAPERBACK

SCHOLASTIC INC.
New York Toronto London Auckland Sydney Tokyo

For
Ilene Balsam and Reggie
Jodi Fine and Buttons
and my own Laurie and the real Misty
because they taught me how to love a puppy
and for
Brian and Michael Gerstein
Ian and Debbie Warren
because they'd love to have a puppy too...

ISBN 0-590-31561-7

12 11 10 9 8 7 6 5 4 3 2 1   3   3 4 5 6/8
Printed in the U.S.A.   11

one

As usual, Mom saved her big announcement for the dinner table. And doctors wonder why kids get nervous stomachs. She looked at all of us, cleared her throat and tapped on her water glass.

"All of us," means me, my father, and my brother Willie. I'm Kimberly Bowman, commonly called Kim except when someone wants my attention immediately, then I'm called all sorts of things. I just started sixth grade, and if the first week is any indication, it's either going to be a great year or a stinky one, no in-betweens.

William Morris Bowman the First is my father. He's in insurance. I don't know why people say that. It sounds like he's in socks or girdles, when all it means is that he sells insurance. He specializes in disasters: fires, floods, automobile crashes, suicides — though we don't have too many of those in Hillside.

William Morris Bowman the Second is called Junior by my grandparents and Willie by everybody else. (My father's called Bill.) He's six years old and in the first grade, and I don't know why they picked him to carry on the family name, except that he's a boy. If it's any indication of his personality, when I talk to him — and believe me, it's only when I have to — I call him Willie the Whiner.

Anyway, Mom said, "I have exciting news. It's something I'm going to do, but it means all of you will have to pitch in and help."

Daddy said, "Please pass the peas," so I figured he had already heard the big announcement.

"I've been offered a full-time job as assistant personnel manager for the Denninger Company, and I'm going to take it." So far she hadn't spoiled my appetite, although I didn't like that remark about all of us pitching in.

"What does full-time mean?" Willie must have been worried, he stopped eating.

"Well, just like Daddy, I'll leave home about

eight-thirty in the morning, but I'll be back about four-thirty."

Willie mashed his peas. He wouldn't eat them anyway because they were green, and he wasn't eating anything green this month. "But Mommy," he started to cry. "Who's going to get me to school?" One of the unmashed peas flew off his plate. "And who's going to take care of me after school?"

Mom was sitting as if she had a ruler straightening her shoulders. She was looking at me and smiling. A piece of my chopped sirloin steak, which is really hamburger with some mushroom sauce over it, stopped moving into my stomach. It was caught in the middle of my ribs.

"Willie, you're very lucky," she said. "You have a big sister in sixth grade. She'll walk you in the morning and wait after school in the playground. So you both will come home together."

Big sister! The piece of meat plopped into my stomach. I knew it was going to bounce around there for a long time. Last Friday night, I wanted to go to the movies with my best friend, Lisa, and Mom told me I was just a kid, too little for night movies.

"Mom." I put my fork down. I even folded my napkin carefully. It was important how

I talked now. If I started yelling and screaming, she would never listen to me. "The sixth grade has lots of activities, after school and everything. This is our last year in Deerfield before we go to Junior High."

She was very calm. "I'm sure there's no activity that you can't take your little brother along to until I get home at four-thirty."

"Take him along!" I couldn't help it. I yelled!

"Don't talk to your mother like that, Kimberly," Daddy said. That's nice, I was glad to see he was listening. Here his wife was going out to work all day, and he just sat there as if it were nothing.

Willie's nose was running. "I don't want to stay with Kim. She's mean to me in front of her friends."

"Mean to you? You're always hanging on my heels, and you're always afraid of something. You never can do anything for yourself." I handed him my napkin. "And wipe your nose — it's dripping."

"Look," Mom was using her no-more-fooling-around voice. "There's no discussion about it. I'm going back to work. It's the kind of job I trained for all those years in college before I got married and had you kids. It's time for me to get back into the field now and do my thing. Besides, we can use extra money around here. Before long we'll have your college to think about, Kim."

COLLEGE! Boy, I'm just a little kid in the sixth grade. I've got years and years and years to go to college. And Willie has even more years.

Daddy put his hand on my wrist. He always says he can read my face for storm clouds. "Cool down, Kim. It won't be so bad. You'll take some books and crayons to keep Willie occupied when he has to go with you."

"And you'll get a baby-sitting salary, too," Mom piped in. Big deal! How was I going to spend money if I always had *him* around? Mom always used to say she remembered just what it felt like to be growing up. She sure got amnesia all of a sudden.

Willie pushed his salad away. Mom picked out a tomato. "Here, Willie, it's red."

"Yech," I said. "Am I going to have to be in charge of his food, too?"

"No, Kim, I'll be home in time for dinner. Besides, the month is almost up. Willie will be eating green foods again." She ruffled his hair. "Won't you, Willie?"

He was sniffing. "I don't know. I might not be able to eat green for the rest of the year."

Who knows what'll happen when Mom isn't

around all day? He'll probably stop eating everything. Then she'll have to use all her salary to take him to a psychiatrist. She's probably making more problems for us than we've got already.

I went back to my chopped steak, though by now the mushroom sauce was cold and congealed in the corner of my plate. I forced myself to eat because I figured I'd better get used to cold meals if Mom was going back to work.

"O.K., O.K.," I said between bites. "But we go to pick up my dog before Mom starts work." It got very quiet.

It's funny about silences. They give me vibrations. I knew this silence wasn't a good one. Daddy wasn't chewing anymore and Mom's shoulders dropped. She was crossing and uncrossing her knees under the table. I could tell, because the tablecloth was pulling.

"Kim, you know that dog business was not a definite promise," she began.

"Not a definite promise!" She wasn't going to get away with that. I pushed my plate back and stood up. "You promised and promised me a dog. You too, Daddy, you know you did."

"It wasn't a promise. I said we'd see," she mumbled.

"No, it was a promise. First, I couldn't have one for years because Willie had all those allergies."

"Well, you know that was true," she said.

"Yeah, but he's had about five thousand shots, and Dr. Stanton said he wasn't allergic to dogs."

"I don't want any more shots."

"Of course not, darling. You won't get any more."

"Then you said I couldn't get a dog until I proved that I was responsible and did chores around the house, like the dishes and picking up my room and stuff."

Silence again. Daddy cleared his throat. "Look, Kim, we're not saying no dog *ever*. But right now Mom's going back to work, and she has to get a schedule set up for the house to run smoothly. A dog would be too much extra work."

"Extra work! But I'm the one who's going to take care of it. Mom, you won't have to do one thing."

"Kim, what are you going to do when you're at school all day? Who will feed it and take it out and watch it until you come home?"

"I'll work it out."

Her shoulders were straight again. "I'm sorry, Kim, not now. I just have too much to get settled to take on a little puppy."

"It'll be *my* puppy. *I'll* be responsible."

She had two red spots on her cheeks. "Like you were responsible for the gerbils you brought home from school that got loose and ran away? And the goldfish you forgot to feed?"

"Gee whiz, I was about eight years old then, Mom." Boy, do one wrong thing and she never lets you forget.

"That's the end, Kim. Sit down and finish supper."

I pulled away from Daddy's hand. "No, I won't. You're mean and unfair. Both of you." I pointed at Mom. "Especially you. You're always telling me a person has to do their own thing and be responsible. How come I'm responsible enough to take care of Willie, but not a puppy?"

"I think you'd better go to your room, Kim." Now Daddy had his firm voice. He acts like he's on your side, but when it gets down to the final crunch, he always sticks up for Mom. Maybe I'd have a better chance if they were divorced. All the books say each parent tries to buy the kids' love by giving them things. I bet then I'd have two puppies.

I flopped onto the bed. Almost everybody I know has a dog. I've wanted one ever since I knew what a dog was. It didn't have to have fancy pedigree papers like Eddie Feeny's down the street. Just a plain puppy that would cuddle up and play and sleep in my room and always take my side. I opened my scrapbook full of dog pictures. I wanted something little, not like a German shepherd or a Labrador retriever. My nose was getting full. Some times I feel sorry when I get into yelling fights with Mom, but not tonight. No matter how she tried to get out of it, she was wrong. They had promised me a dog.

And this year especially. My friend Lisa had been away all summer. The minute I saw her, I knew we weren't going to be the same kind of friends we had always been. She had grown about three inches, and she was walking hunched over to hide her new front. Now I walk hunched over because I don't want anyone to see that I don't have anything to hide.

The first fifteen minutes we spent together she combed her hair the whole time. She told me I had two zits on my face and that my mother should take me to have my hair styled. It was too babyish for a sixth-grader.

When I got out part of my collection of

paper dolls, she forgot about her hair for a while. Then she said paper dolls were baby stuff and she thought we should be interested in boys this year. I told her if she had to be around Willie the Whiner all the time, she would hate boys. She said brothers didn't count as boys!

I have a picture of a really cute toy poodle with a ribbon in its hair. I hear they're very nervous, temperamental dogs. If there's anything we don't need around this house, it's more nerves.

I pushed the scrapbook off the bed and hugged my pillow. See, if I had a little puppy right now, I could be telling it all these things, and then I wouldn't care about Mom or Daddy or Lisa. I might even be able to bear Willie. Though, of course, if I had the puppy right now, I wouldn't be lying up here on my bed feeling sorry for myself.

two

Mom's first day of work arrived. She was dressed up in a pleated skirt and a blouse and a wool jacket. She had her make-up fixed just like she does on Saturday night when they go out. She looked nice, but I wouldn't tell her.

Willie the Whiner was crying. "What if Kim doesn't find me in the yard?"

"Of course she will. Tell him, Kim."

"But there's lots of kids, Mommy, and the first grade gets out a different door."

"Kim, please tell him that you'll find him."

"Oh, I'll find you. How can I miss? You'll be the only kid whose nose is running."

"Make her stop saying that. She's going to be mean to me."

"Kimberly Bowman, PL-EA-SE!" Mom was screeching. I'll bet if her boss saw how she couldn't even handle two little kids, he wouldn't put her in charge of a whole personnel department.

Daddy walked in. "Everybody ready? Let's go. We'll all leave the house together."

"What's going to happen on a day when Willie is sick? Am I going to have to stay home?"

"Don't be silly," said Mom. "I've spoken to Mrs. Snider. She'll come over in emergencies."

Our station wagon had had a carburetor attack in the middle of the summer. At least that's what Mother called it. Only it had never recuperated. That was another reason for this job, she said. To save up for a new car. Meanwhile she was driving Daddy to his office, then she would take his car so she could get home early. Daddy would car-pool home with people from his office.

It seemed to me that an awful lot of people were being inconvenienced just so she could do her thing.

I handed her a newspaper article. "Maybe

you'll have time to read this on your coffee break. You do get a coffee break, don't you?"

Daddy smiled. "Your mother's an executive. Executives don't get coffee breaks or punch a clock."

"Well, do executives go to the bathroom? Maybe you can read it then."

"Oh, don't be silly, Kim. Of course I'll read it. Give it to me." She put it in her bag. It was from our local paper — an announcement from the Union County Animal Shelter that they had many puppies that needed a good home. You were advised to come between the hours of nine and five. If homes weren't found, the dogs would be put to sleep.

Mom's not mean, even though she's doing her thing. If she reads that puppies are going to be put to sleep if they don't get a good home, I'm sure she'll reconsider.

I walked Willie right to the door of the first grade. Miss Foster met us. "Your mother told me she was going back to work, Kim. I think it's great. And don't worry about Willie. We have lots of fun in class, don't we, Willie?" Why should I worry about Willie? As far as I was concerned, if she thought the situation was so wonderful, she could take Willie home with her and watch him till summer vacation.

There are two sixth grades. Lisa and I are in the same one this year. I hurried to meet her. She was standing with Mary Jo and Sandy. They had skirts on.

"Why are you wearing a skirt, Lisa?"

"Because." There was that comb again.

"I bet your hair falls out from all that combing."

She swished her hair across her shoulders. It sure looked blonder to me than it had before the summer. "It wouldn't hurt you to comb your hair, Kimberly Bowman."

"I did."

"When, last week?"

The other girls giggled. I scraped my sneaker against the locker. It wasn't like Lisa to be mean. Especially to me. We had made special string friendship bracelets before she left for camp. We had divided a piece of string and tied the halves around each other's wrists. You're supposed to leave it on until it falls apart by itself. Mom yelled at me all summer to get rid of that dirty piece of cord. But I never took it off, even when we went swimming at Bradley Beach.

Lisa's arm was bare. Mine still had its bracelet. I didn't want to ask her where her bracelet was in front of the other girls. It seemed funny for one half of the same string to disintegrate before the other.

Well, one thing that was going to be fabulous this year was English. Mrs. Brock announced an open reading program for qualified students. I was really excited when I saw my name on the list.

I whispered to Lisa, "Isn't that great? You're on it, too. What are you going to read first?"

If she kept swishing her hair back and forth like that, people were going to think something was the matter with her neck.

"Oh, I'm not going to have time for extra reading. And guess what? My mom's taking me shopping this afternoon."

"Oh." My mom was working that afternoon.

She pinched my back. "Listen, do you want to go with us?" Now that was like the old Lisa.

"Willie the Whiner, remember?"

"Oh, darn. Well, I'll call you when I get home and tell you what I get, O.K.?"

I shook my head yes. I felt better about Lisa. Mrs. Brock handed me a book of poems. "Try some of these on for size, will you, Kim? We want to stretch your mind this year. Let me know how you make out." Well, at least

I could read after school. But first — well, it wouldn't hurt if Willie and I went home by way of the pound. Just to see the puppies they had. Then if Mom read the article, we could tell her at dinner, and maybe tomorrow we could stop before she went to work and get one.

There was still that business about feeding it while I was in school. If I was smart enough to be in an open advanced reading program, I should be smart enough to figure something out. Maybe I'd come across an idea in one of the books. Writers are pretty smart people. I put the poetry book in my book bag and went out to find Willie.

He was sitting on the grass. "Where were you? I've been here a long time."

When Willie's in a mood, a blink of the eye can be a long time. "Don't start whining. My class just got out. Come on." I yanked him to his feet and pulled him through the gate.

"I'm hungry. This isn't the way home. Aren't we going to have a snack?"

"No, not yet. I want to go into town for a while."

"But I'm thirsty. Mommy always has a snack for me after school."

"Well, Mom is now busy worrying about snacks for all the factory workers at Den-

16

ninger's." His nose and eyes scrunched together. I knew what that meant.

"If you cry, Willie, I'll smack you."

His face went back into place. "Where are we going?"

"I want to go past the pound to see what kind of pups they've got."

"Mommy said you couldn't get a dog."

"She didn't say I couldn't ever. She just said right now I couldn't get a dog."

"Well, I'm going to tell that you went to look for a dog and you didn't even get me a snack."

It amazes me. Willie has this thick black hair that flops in his eyes. When you do see his eyes, they're bright and sparkling. People think he's adorable. Until he opens his mouth.

Now take me. I have brown hair and brown eyes. The hair's a little stringy, but I have a pretty good personality, if I do say so myself. Wouldn't you think I should have Willie's hair, which always seems to shine even when it's dirty? Also, those long eyelashes of his are absolutely wasted on such a whiner.

The Union County Animal Shelter. We could hear barking. Willie let go of my hand and pushed the door open ahead of me. "Let's go, Kim. I hear them."

Phew! What a smell. I noticed that before

I could even focus on anything else. It was something like the monkey cage at the zoo. But no animals in sight. Just a desk with a guy on the telephone. The dogs must be in a back room. They were certainly making enough noise. Willie started sneezing. I handed him a tissue. "Please, Willie, no allergy attacks now."

He held his nose. "P.U.!"

"Hey, mister?" The guy kept talking. He waved to us as if to say "Just a minute."

I tried again. "Mister?"

He held one hand over the mouthpiece. "Just a minute, kid." I hate when people call me kid. And I hate when people keep you waiting just because you are a kid. I didn't think the county should leave a person in charge who was going to keep people waiting.

Finally! "O.K., what can I do ya for?" I knew he never had Miss Purcell for English, talking like that.

"Well, speak up. Dog or cat? We got big ones, little ones, flat ones, tall ones, skinny ones, hungry ones, hairy ones, what'll ya have?"

He sounded like he was selling used cars or something, not live, breathing animals. He unlocked the back door. Cages were piled one on top of another. As we walked in, the dogs stopped for a minute and then started barking again.

"P.U., it stinks more in here." Willie was still holding his nose.

The dogs got quiet. I had never seen a worse bunch in my life. They didn't look anything like my scrapbook pictures — or the dogs for sale in the Doggy Palace that have pedigree papers and cost about two hundred dollars. These dogs were dirty and their fur was matted, and some had eyes as runny as Willie's nose. Some could hardly lift their heads. They didn't look like they had strength to even bark. Maybe a machine had been doing the barking. I couldn't imagine any of them lying across my toes keeping me warm while I read my advanced reading books.

"Most of these are old and sick," the guy said. He reached through a cage and patted the head of a terrier that had bald patches on it. "Shh, come on, old fella, these here kids ain't gonna hurt ya." His voice was pretty gentle. I guess these dogs don't care about bad English.

"You had an ad in the paper for puppies," I said.

"Yeah, we always run that. But we don't have any today."

"Will you be getting any fresh ones in?"

asked Willie. He hadn't sniffed once since we were here with the dogs.

"Sure. People bring 'em in all the time. Their dogs have a litter and they can't take care of 'em."

"Could you let us know when you get some pups in that we'd be able to adopt?" I asked.

"Yeah, we want a new one. Not old broken ones like these."

"Willie." I smacked his shoulder. "That's not nice. How would you like someone to say that about you?" Actually I had been thinking the same thing a few minutes ago.

"Well, I could give ya a call. Leave ya number."

I tore off a piece of notebook paper and printed my number carefully. "Please ask for Kimberly Bowman when you call."

He put it in his pocket. "O.K. My name's Norman. Ya got your mom's permission, don't ya? We can't let no dogs outa here without a adult."

"Our mom . . ." I clapped my hand over Willie's mouth.

"Sure we have permission. What do you think? How could we take a dog home without permission?"

"O.K. And remember, ya pay ten bucks, 'cause we give the pup its first shot."

"Shot? You mean dogs get shots, too?"

"Quiet, Willie. Please call us as soon as some puppies come in."

"I'll put ya on the list. There's a waitin' list for healthy pups, ya know."

"I really appreciate it." I took Willie's hand.

The dogs started barking and jumping and scratching against their cages as we left. I felt kind of bad. It was as if they had tried to be quiet and on their best behavior so they'd get adopted, and now they knew we were leaving without choosing any of them.

Norman was scratching his face. I yelled above the barks. "Uh, listen, don't forget to ask for Kimberly Bowman and, uh, if I'm not home, don't say who's calling."

"Oh, yeah, why not?"

I thought fast. "Because it's a surprise. I mean, my mother knows, but it's a surprise for our other brother. A puppy for his birthday."

"We don't have another bro — " My hand just made it across Willie's mouth again. "Shh," I whispered, "I'll tell you later."

We could hear the dogs barking after us halfway down the block. It sounded like crying.

three

Mom wasn't home yet. The key was under the front mat. I told Mom that's the most conspicuous place to leave it. Everybody leaves a key under the mat. Daddy says that's why a burglar wouldn't look there. He'd try to figure out an exotic hiding place, like under the drainpipe. Besides, Daddy says we might as well just leave our front door wide open, because there's nothing to steal.

The house was really quiet. Empty. Usually I know when Mom's home, even if she's quiet. I get her vibrations.

I poured Willie some milk. "I want chocolate." I stirred in chocolate. He took a sip and made a face. "It's not sweet enough." I gave him a little more. Another face. "It's too sweet."

"Look, Whiner!" I pointed the dripping spoon at him. "You can pull all this baby stuff with Mom, but I'm not going to put up with it."

"Where are you going?" he asked.

"To my room."

"Can I come with you?"

"Yes, finish your milk and rinse the glass."

It was peculiar to find the beds unmade at four o'clock in the afternoon. Things were so hectic this morning that Mom's plan for all of us to make our own beds didn't work out. I straightened mine. Willie followed me into the room.

"Look, Willie, if you're good and help me make the beds before Mom gets home, I'll let you look at the dog scrapbook."

I really didn't have to make the beds; it wasn't in my agreement with Mom. I figured I should store up all the extra points I could to prove how responsible I was.

We finished and went back to my room to look through the scrapbook. "Oh, look at this collie!" Willie pointed to a picture of Lassie.

"Too big." I tried to turn the page.

"I think it would be great to have a collie. Then we could put it on TV commercials."

"Look, Willie, this dog is supposed to stay home with me and be my pet. I don't want it running around on TV."

"Who said it's going to be your dog?"

"Well, it is." I saw the crumple begin. "You can help take care of it." He started sniffing. "All right, all right, we'll share him." Willie smiled. Under my breath I said the dog would still belong to me. Willie gets tired of things very quickly.

"Do you think anybody brought a puppy in since we left there?" he asked. I had been wondering myself.

"Let's call and see." I dialed the pound. "Hi, is this Norman? This is Kim Bowman. My brother and I were wondering if any pups came in yet?"

"Listen, kid," he blasted through the phone. "Nobody brought no pups in yet. Don't call me, I'll call ya." And SLAM went the receiver.

I shrugged at Willie. "No dogs yet. He'll call us."

It was way after five when we heard Mom. "Quick, somebody, I need help." Willie beat me down the stairs. "You're late, Mommy, I'm hungry. Guess what happened today?"

I followed quickly. I didn't want him slipping about the animal shelter. I didn't have to worry. Mom was in such a state, I don't think she would have heard anyway.

"Oh, Kim, here." She handed me a big bucket of Kentucky Fried Chicken with french fries and biscuits. Boy, if we were going to eat like this every night, her working wouldn't be so bad.

"Willie, please run out to the car. I picked up Daddy's shirts at the laundry, they're on the front seat. I'm exhausted." She threw her jacket around one of the kitchen chairs. It missed and landed on the floor, just like mine does when I'm in a hurry. "I think every unemployed person in the state of New Jersey came to Denninger's today for a job!" She pulled some frozen string beans out of the freezer. "Put a pot of water on to boil for the string beans, will you, honey?"

I picked up her jacket without asking her how she could be so careless, the way she usually asks me. Willie came in with the shirts. "We had art this afternoon, Mommy. I couldn't cut out on the black lines, because my scissors weren't sharp. And I have to have my milk money for next week."

"Please, Willie, just a minute." She handed me paper plates.

"We'll have a picnic tonight, and then we won't have to wash dishes." The phone rang. "It's Nannie," I said.

She grabbed the phone out of my hand. "Yes, Mom, everything was great. Just a minute. Kim, turn the gas down, the water's boiling over. Mom, I can't talk now, I just walked in. I'll call you later."

She turned on the oven and put the chicken in to keep it warm. "I'll be right down. I've just got to get out of these clothes and wash my face." She kicked off her shoes and left them at the bottom of the stairs. I saw ball-point ink on her second finger. She must have been doing a lot of writing.

Willie followed at her heels, still whining about his school day. She kept saying, "O.K., Willie. Yes, honey. Don't worry about it, sweetie." If she would just tell him once to shut up, he might stop whining. I should tell her how good he was at the pound. As a matter of fact, he hadn't whined since he finished his chocolate milk.

She yelled from upstairs. "Look at all these dirty towels in the bathroom. Can't you kids remember to throw them in the laundry basket?" I waited, but she didn't say anything about the beds. Well, that's the last time I was going to do them if she wasn't even going to notice.

Daddy came in. He was whistling. Sure, it had just been a normal day for him. He walked into the kitchen. "Hi, Kim, Mom home?" He always asked about her first.

"She's upstairs," I said.

"How'd it go today? Willie give you any trouble?" He gave me a hug. Daddy always smelled as good when he came home as he had when he left in the morning.

"Oh, Willie wasn't too bad, except he was nervous because he had to wait two minutes for me after school. And I made the beds for Mom and she didn't even notice."

"Oh, I'm sure she noticed, Kim. Remember, the first week or so it's going to be hard for everybody until we get used to this new routine. It's especially hard on Mom."

I bit my tongue so I wouldn't say that nobody told her to go to work. And there was no sense bringing up a discussion about puppies. I was pretty sure that she had never read the article I had given her.

Norman didn't call the next day, or the next, or the next. Over the weekend Mom made all kinds of casseroles and put them in the freezer. She wrote out instructions about what time they were to be put into the oven for warming.

Daddy helped her with the laundry. We all pitched in. Even Willie had to fold towels, which is my favorite job because they come out so warm and fluffy from the drier. I got stuck sorting socks and practically went blind trying to get Daddy's blues and blacks matched.

Willie started sneezing, and Mom got frazzled because she hadn't had a chance to dust under the beds. "That's all I need," she said. "To have dust start his allergies all over again."

Daddy told her to relax. "You're not a machine," he said. "So the house isn't perfect. Don't worry about it."

I was getting frazzled myself, what with watching Willie every afternoon, waiting for Norman to call, and having Lisa act so strange. Nobody seemed to worry about me.

The next few days went a little more smoothly. Mom hired a lady to come in and do the heavy cleaning once a week. She felt better when she didn't see any dust under the beds.

Lisa and I ate lunch together every day. But she always included Amy, and they seemed to have more to talk about than I did.

On Thursday Lisa whispered that she had a special announcement to make at lunchtime. Amy giggled. After the last special announcement I had heard, I decided to wait before I got excited.

"My mother's on the PTA committee, and they hired a teacher for Friday afternoons and we're going to have disco dancing."

"Fabulous!" yelled Amy.

I wasn't so sure. But I didn't want to act like a jerk. "How come disco dancing?" I asked Lisa.

"Because the PTA wants us socially ready for junior high and high school and college. You know. This way we'll learn all the latest dances."

Between my mother and the PTA, I was going to be a college graduate before I had a chance to finish sixth-grade reading.

"Are the boys going to sign up?" asked Amy.

"That's the problem. The boys don't want to. But if we can get Doug to come, all the others will follow him."

It looked like my only hope was that Doug wouldn't go, so the girls wouldn't have anybody to dance with and the whole thing would fall through.

Lisa covered her mouth with her hand and

whispered so Amy wouldn't hear. "Why don't you come over this afternoon? We haven't had any private talks this year."

I had been waiting for her to ask me. Last year I wouldn't have needed an invitation. I was always there, or she was at my house.

"Willie, remember?" I said.

"Oh, pooh. So what. He can watch TV, can't he?"

So after school, Willie and I walked to Lisa's. We settled him in front of the TV with a big bowl of popcorn that we'd popped over the stove.

"Doesn't he have any friends he can play with?" she asked.

"You know how sick he was when he was a baby. There're no little kids on our block his age, and now that my mother works, she doesn't want him someplace he'll have to be picked up and driven to. And you know what a whiner he is."

We went up to her room. She showed me all the new clothes her mother had bought her. I had to speak up. "My mother's going to take me shopping this Saturday," I said. The truth was Mom had wanted to take me, but I already had plenty of jeans and shirts. I didn't know Lisa and the other girls were going to make such a big fuss over clothes this year. The boys still dressed the same.

"Don't forget to get some skirts. If disco dancing goes through, we're all going to wear skirts." She twirled around the room holding an imaginary skirt out in the air. She sure looked dippy. I spoke up quickly.

"I saw a jumper in the paper, and my mother said I could have it. You can wear it with a sweater or a blouse." I wasn't going to let her think I didn't know anything. Lucky that Mom had showed it to me the other night when she was looking through a department-store catalog. But I'd wait until I was sure they were going to have disco dancing. I didn't want to be stuck with a dumb jumper.

"Kim, I have a really important secret. Want to hear?"

"Sure."

"Cross your heart and hope to die."

I did — cross my heart, that is; I never hope to die. "Before you tell me the secret, Lisa, what happened to your string bracelet?" I pointed to her empty wrist.

"Oh, that. You mean you still have yours?" She grabbed my wrist. "Ech, it's filthy. You should really get rid of it. Up at my camp they didn't do baby things like that."

She hadn't thought it was so babyish last June. Did that mean she cut it off? That was against the rules! It was supposed to fall off by itself, and you were supposed to write down the date to see if your best friend's fell off near the same time. Well, maybe she cheated, but I wasn't going to. A promise was a promise.

"Anyway, Kim, I don't want to talk about string bracelets. I want to tell you about Mark."

"What about Mark?" Maybe she knew something really good, like he had tripped and gotten fouled on the basketball court.

"Well, Doug thinks I like *him*. But I'm really going to like Mark this year. Mark calls me up every night."

This was the secret? I thought it was going to be something special. She really meant it when she said she was going to take up boys this year.

"Well, if I thought you were going to act like this, I wouldn't have told you." Lisa was miffed because I wasn't excited about her secret.

I tried. "I think Mark is great, Lisa. Really, he's much cuter than Doug."

"Do you think so?" I didn't think either

one of them was cute, but if it made her happy . . .

"Now do you want to hear *my* secret?" I asked.

"I guess so."

I told her about the pound and Norman and how we — Willie and I — were waiting to hear about the puppy.

"Oh." She swung her hair around. "Is he cute?"

"The puppy? I don't know. We haven't seen what we're getting yet."

"Not the puppy. Norman, the guy in charge."

"Norman! Who cares about Norman?"

Lisa turned her back and grabbed her hairbrush. She didn't seem to care. I guess you have to keep real important secrets inside yourself. Once you tell somebody, they can take it, pick it up, shake it out, and drop it like it's a big nothing.

"Why don't you try him again?" she said.

"Who?"

"Norman. You're not home, are you? Maybe a pup came in today and you won't even know."

I guess Lisa did care. We went into her mother's bedroom to use the phone. He answered right away.

"Hello, Norman, this is . . ."

"Yeah, yeah. Kimberly Bowman. I figured it was time for ya to call."

"Anything come in yet?" I crossed my fingers to Lisa. She crossed hers back.

"Well, this here lady called, and her dog had a litter about six weeks ago, and she sold all except two."

"Is she bringing them in?"

"Well, as a matter of fact, she's supposed to come in on Monday."

I waved a victory fist in the air and started to bounce on the bed. "Oh, Norman, that's terrific! Please save us one. We'll come right after school."

Lisa was saying something. "What kind of pup? Ask him what kind of pup."

"What kind are they, Norman?"

"I ain't seen them, but the lady tells me they're mostly beagle."

"Mostly beagle!" I yelled to Lisa.

"Hey, kid?"

"What, Norman?"

"A couple of things. I don't like to bring this up, but ya know I got a long list waiting on these pups."

My heart fell. It really did. If I didn't have a bottom to my body, I think it would have fallen right on the bed.

"So people usually take care of me for puttin' 'em on the top of the list."

"I'll take care of you, Norman." I shrugged my shoulders to Lisa, who wanted to know what he was saying.

"O.K., great. Remember, the shelter charges ten bucks for the pup and the first shot. And a little somethin' extra for me, for puttin' ya on top of the list. And don't forget, an adult has to come in with ya."

"Come in with me? Can't I just bring a note from my mother?"

"No can do, kiddo. The rules is a pup can't leave the premises with no minor kids."

"O.K., Norman. I'll come with an adult. On Monday. I swear. I promise. Please, Norman. Don't give the puppy to anybody else."

"I'll hold till Monday, four o'clock."

I hung up and flopped across the bed. "I've got it. I've got it!"

"What did he want?"

I repeated the rest of the conversation to Lisa. She sat up. "Aha, when he says 'something extra,' it means he wants money. A tip for himself."

"That's not legal."

"Yeah. But what are you going to do? Once we were in this restaurant and they said they were filled up, and my father gave the waiter a tip and we got a table."

Lisa was right. I had seen my father give plenty of extra money tips for things, too. Who could I tell? I doubt if the governor would listen to a sixth-grader.

"How much do you think I have to give him?"

"I don't know. How much do you have? And what are you going to do about the adult?"

That was a toughie. I could forge a note from my mother, but now I had to forge a whole mother.

I tossed a pillow at her. "I'll think about it tomorrow."

I ducked as the pillow came back to me. "That sounds familiar," Lisa said.

"Advanced reading," I answered, this time catching her right in the stomach and throwing her off the bed.

"Ouch, you rat — I know, Scarlett O'Hara, *Gone with the Wind*." I ducked and the pillow knocked an ashtray off the night table.

"Lisa," a voice called from the kitchen. "What's all that noise? I see Willie Bowman here. Is Kim upstairs with you?" It was Lisa's mother.

We jumped off the bed giggling, and straightened the spread. "By the way, Kimberly Bowman." Lisa picked up the ashtray. "I hope you know I'm going with you Monday."

I shook her hand. "Great!"

"I wouldn't miss it for anything. I can't wait to see how you're going to get this puppy."

"Oh, you'll see it, all right. And Lisa, don't bother to wear one of your skirts. Puppies aren't really interested in clothes." I ran out the door as she aimed another pillow at me. I was trying to act confident, but right then, I couldn't see how I was going to get the puppy either!

four

On the way home I tried to make a list in my head of all the things I would have to do before Monday. "Willie, as soon as we're home I want you to bring me all the money you've got."

"What for?"

"For the puppy, of course. Now don't waste time asking questions. Just do it."

I ran right up to my room and Willie went for his piggy bank. I had six dollars saved up. I would have had four more dollars, but I had bought a rock record at the end of the summer. Darn it! I didn't even play the thing anymore. And you could hear the songs free all the time on the radio. Sometimes Mom is right. She always says to think carefully before spending money. Of course, I didn't know at the time that I was going to have to be responsible for all the finances involved in getting a puppy.

Willie opened his bank. He had seventy-five cents. He gave it to me but held one hand behind his back.

"What do you have back there, Willie?"

"It's something special, but if it's for the puppy, I'll let you have it."

"Do you have more money? Quick, give it here." I grabbed his hand and opened his fist. There was a stack of baseball cards.

"Baseball cards!" I let them drop to the floor. "We need money and you give me baseball cards! What the heck am I supposed to do with them?"

He had tears in his eyes. "I heard you tell Lisa that Norman wanted something extra, so I thought you could give him my baseball cards. I'm only missing two Yankees, and maybe I can get them by tomorrow if you give me back twenty-five cents so I can buy some more bubble gum this afternoon."

His tears were two little streams down his cheeks. Sometimes I am really a selfish, unkind rat. "Blow, Willie." I gave him one of my hankies. It said Friday instead of•Wednesday, but I was so mixed up today I even had my Saturday underpants on.

"Sit down, Willie." I patted the bed and bent down to pick up his cards. "That was a terrific sacrifice you were about to make. But it's not necessary. We'll get the pup without your baseball cards. Let's just think for a minute."

I jumped up. "The PTA money."

"My milk money." Willie's mind was on the same track as mine. Mother had laid out the envelopes carefully. We were supposed to bring them in tomorrow. Willie's milk money for the week was a dollar and a half. The PTA dues were two dollars a parent. That made four dollars more. We had twelve dollars and twenty-five cents; ten dollars for the dog and two dollars and twenty-five cents extra for Norman.

Next week I would get my baby-sitting money from Mom and Daddy. They were going to pay me three dollars a week, once a month. So I could replace the PTA dues and no one would ever know.

"Are you sure you won't miss your milk this week?" I asked.

"Nah. They only let you have white milk, and I'm not going to have any white foods this month." Willie was more accurate about the changing of the months than a calendar.

The money problem was solved. Now where was I going to get an adult and a place to keep the pup?

I thought I'd never fall asleep that night. It shows what worrying can do to a person. Mom always says the house could fall on my head and it wouldn't wake me up.

In the morning she asked if I was all right. "You look a little pale today, Kim."

"I'm fine." She was the perfect personnel manager. She couldn't have me sick; who would take care of Willie? I wasn't about to be sick anyway. I had too much to do.

When I got to school I found a note in my locker. "I can't talk to you during class because my mother says if I get detention once more, she's going to punish me for a month. Wait after school. URGENT! THIS IS NO JOKE!!" It was signed by Lisa.

After school she handed me a dollar and a half. "I was saving up for some strawberry lip gloss, but I guess this is a little more important." She ran her tongue over her lips. "I can keep them shiny like this until you pay me back."

"Thanks, Lisa." This meant I had one dollar and fifty cents extra, in case Norman didn't think his tip was big enough. "Your lips really look great the way they are. Just as wet as lip gloss." Privately I thought it was gooky. Why were wet lips supposed to make you look kissable? She'd probably wear the skin off her mouth licking at them all day.

"And look at this." She pulled out a section of newspaper.

"What's that?"

"It's from the classified section of the Hillside paper."

"But I can't get a job. I have to take care of Willie."

"Not for you, silly. It has people in here who are looking for jobs. Once my father needed a typist, and he got one from the paper."

"Oh." I still didn't understand.

"Look, you need someone to take care of the dog, right?"

Now I got it. I pulled the paper from her hand. Willie came over to us. "Go on the swings, Willie. Lisa and I are looking for something."

"Is it about the dog?" he asked.

"Yes." I gave him a shove. "Now go."

We searched the columns and circled a few ads. Then I called out: "Let's go home,

Willie!" The three of us ran all the way. When we got there, I made the calls. A Mr. Connors had an ad in for odd jobs around the house. I asked if he would watch a dog. He said that wasn't an odd job, it was a full-time job, and hung up. Three ladies had ads in for baby-sitting. One hung up, one wasn't home, and one called me a fresh kid for suggesting she dog-sit.

There was one ad on the bottom. "Elderly lady will watch your plants while you go on vacation; knit beautiful sweaters; baby-sit at my home. Any odd job to help me live on Social Security."

"That doesn't sound so good. If she says elderly, she must be a hundred. No one wants to admit that they're old," said Lisa.

"Well, I'm going to try anyway. There're no more ads left."

The phone rang five times. I was just about to hang up when I heard a sweet voice. "Can I help you? This is Mrs. Macvey."

I crossed my fingers and said, "This is Kim Bowman. I sure hope you can."

Ten minutes later I hung up with Mrs. Macvey's address. I was dripping wet. Willie and Lisa were jumping up and down. "What did she say? What did she say?"

"She said we can come over and talk."

Willie and Lisa hugged each other. Lisa seemed as excited as we were, and she hadn't licked her lips to make them shiny all afternoon. "I wish I could go with you," she said, "but I've got dumb ballet in a half-hour. And my mother drives the car pool. She'll kill me if I'm late. Call me as soon as you know anything."

Mrs. Macvey was sitting on her porch in a straight-back chair. She lived about two blocks from school but in the opposite direction from our house. It was sort of an old-fashioned house, and I hoped she was insured, because her porch steps were a disaster. Paint was peeling near the front door. She stood up, and I was surprised that she was just a little taller than I was.

"Pleased to meet you, Kim. Just call me Mrs. Mac," she said. I explained that I needed a place to keep my dog until I could talk my mother into letting it come home. There was no sense in lying to Mrs. Mac. Besides, looking right into her eyes gave me a feeling of confidence. And she was really listening to me. Not as if I were a baby. She wore a big apron. It smelled kind of sweet, as if she had dried flowers in her pockets. I figured she might say no, but she didn't look like she would tell.

She invited us in. She didn't have any carpeting on her floors, just some little scatter rugs here and there. Her lamps were kind of funny-looking, with big ruffled skirts on them. We went into the kitchen. There was black-and-white linoleum on the floor, and her sink was the real old kind, with the pipes showing underneath it. There were plants all over the place.

She wore glasses, but I could see that her eyes were very blue. I think she was old enough to be a grandma — probably even a great-grandma — but she wasn't like ours. We call Mom's mother "Nannie Marion" and our grandfather "Poppie." We see a lot of them except in the winter when they go to Florida to live in their condominium. Poppie plays golf, but he still goes to business part-time, and Nannie Marion is an interior decorator. She picks out furniture and carpeting and tells people what color to paint their walls. She wears dress-up clothes almost all the time and her hair doesn't have a speck of gray. She could really do a job in Mrs. Mac's house.

Willie must have been reading my mind because he said, "Do you think Mrs. Mac is very poor?"

It was lucky she had gone to the sink and

was running the water, so she didn't hear him.

"I don't know. Why?"

"Because she has those little rugs and her sink has funny faucets."

"They're not funny, just old. Not modern. They're probably antiques." I really should have Nannie Marion look at them. They might be very valuable. It was crazy, but Nannie always told me that her rich customers liked old things. The older they were, the more they cost. Yet poor people who had all the old junk wanted new stuff.

Mrs. Mac wiped her glasses on her apron. "I don't know about taking care of a puppy. People bring me their plants to take care of, and sometimes I baby-sit with tiny babies for a few hours. A pup might be too much for me."

"We'll be here every morning," I promised, "and right after school and on Saturdays and Sundays, after Sunday school."

"How much do you think you could pay?" she asked. "It's not that I like to talk about money, but it's hard to make ends meet on Social Security."

"Well . . ." I thought quickly. I was getting three dollars a week for taking care of Willie. That didn't sound like too much. But

I had a birthday coming up, and I could ask for money instead of presents. Besides, I was hoping that Mom wouldn't last long at her job. She had a big corn on her little toe because the high heels she wore to the office were pinching her feet.

"I could pay six dollars a week. And I'll pay for the puppy food, too," I added.

"Puppies need a lot of medical care, shots and things," she said. "I know. We had all sorts of pups and cats around when my children were little."

"Where are your children?" asked Willie.

"Oh, they're all grown up and moved away, and they have children that are grown up and moved away. I stayed put right here where I've been most of my life — though now my oldest daughter is after me to close up the house and move in with her."

"I'll get the money," I said, "don't worry about that. And Willie and I can shop and do errands for you."

"Yeah, we can help you take care of plants. I know how to water," he said.

"Well, I don't know if I like fooling your mother," she said.

"It isn't really fooling. Mom will love the idea of the puppy."

"Yeah," said Willie. "Besides, she didn't

say Kim could never have it, just not right now."

"But," I added, "if we bring it home in a few weeks all trained, she'll have to say yes."

Mrs. Mac smiled at me and then patted Willie. For once I was glad he had such nice hair and eyes and looked adorable.

"I guess we could give it a try. It might be nice to have a pup around here again and some kids. Also show my daughter in Ohio that I'm not such a helpless old lady."

My heart jumped. She was going to do it. I must be the greatest persuader on the eastern seaboard. Maybe I could rent myself out to the U.N. We had a three-way shake of hands, Willie, me, and Mrs. Mac. Willie and I waved and started home. I wanted to hop into my bed and sleep for a week. Negotiations make you more tired than any old ballet class.

five

Daddy gave me six dollars on Saturday for the two weeks I had been baby-sitting. So that gave me nineteen dollars and seventy-five cents counting everything, even Lisa's lip gloss money. I thought that would take care of all our expenses and I could even start to repay the PTA money next week.

Every chance I got, I poured Willie a glass of milk and forced him to drink it. I felt guilty about using his milk money. I didn't want his bones to start crumbling because he wasn't getting his morning milk in school.

I called Mrs. Mac on the phone and went over our plan. She agreed to meet Willie and me at the pound on Monday. "Remember," she said, "I'll help you, but I won't tell any lies for you."

"You won't have to," I said. Ask me no questions, I'll tell you no lies. I'd just make sure that nobody asked Mrs. Mac any questions.

I went to the bathroom about fifteen times Monday morning. Being nervous does that to me sometimes. I prayed nothing would go wrong. The day dragged on and on. Once I thought I had lost the money, but it had gotten caught in my pocket with some tissues.

First thing in the morning I had whispered to Lisa. "Today's the day. Don't forget, you're going with me this afternoon."

"This afternoon?" She started combing her hair again. She had really picked up some bad habits at camp. I moved back so I wouldn't get slapped with her hair, because she'd fling it back over her shoulder when she finished combing.

"The pound. The dog, Lisa. This afternoon."

"Oh, the dog. I forgot all about it."

"Forgot?" How could she forget?

"Well, maybe I didn't forget, but we're all going to Jane's house." She whispered in my ear. "The boys are supposed to come over." That was the dumbest thing I ever heard of.

Last week she had given up her lip gloss, and today she didn't even want to go with me to see the puppy she was helping to buy. Just wait until she did want to see it. I'd make her wait a long, long time. I'd tell her to go look at the boys instead.

It felt like three school days instead of one, but finally it was time to get Willie. We ran all the way to the pound. Mrs. Mac was outside waiting for us. Thank goodness she was reliable. You never could tell. We had just met her a couple of days ago. Lisa I knew practically my whole entire life, and I couldn't count on her from one moment to the next.

"Hi, Mrs. Mac. Just wait right outside for us. It won't take a minute."

"O.K., Kim," she said.

I crossed my fingers. If she was outside, Norman couldn't ask her any questions.

Willie and I walked into the office alone. "Where's the dog? Where is it?" asked Willie, looking all around. There were none to be seen. I looked at the wall clock. It was only three-thirty. Norman couldn't have given it away yet.

"Oh, Norman, you promised." I said. "It isn't even anywhere near four o'clock yet." I could hear barks from behind the closed office doors. I wondered which dogs had survived the weekend.

"Hold your horses, hold your horses. Where's your mother?"

"Work . . ." I pinched Willie before he could finish and said quickly, "Our grandmother's here with us."

Norman looked as if he didn't believe me.

"You said an adult, and our mother works."

"Yeah," said Willie, "that's what I was going to say. Our mother works." It was lucky that Willie was a fast catcher-on. Otherwise he would be black and blue all over when I got through with him.

I waved through the window at Mrs. Mac. She waved back. "That's our grandmother," I said to Norman.

He looked suspicious. "Oh, yeah, why don't she come in with ya?"

My darling Willie saved the day. "Allergies!" he said. "She'll sneeze if she smells all the dogs in this place."

Mrs. Mac waved again and blew Willie a kiss.

"O.K., O.K., so that's your grandmother. Now where's the money?" He believed us! I held out the ten dollars. Norman kept his palm open. I gave him two dollars and twenty-five cents more. I had decided that was a big enough tip. "For you," I said.

"Two dollars and twenty-five cents?" squeaked Norman. "You sure you can spare it?"

"No, I really can't, but it's something extra because you've been so nice to us." I used my most sarcastic voice, but my knees were shaking. "Now can we have him?"

"On the floor, behind the desk." Norman was recounting the money. "And it's a she. Here's your receipt. Had one shot already for distemper, leptospirosis, and hepatitis. Take her to the vet before the week's over. If anything's wrong with her, bring her back. That's the state rules."

I really wasn't listening. There she was. Just a rolled-up ball of black and white. Willie said, "Oh, can I touch her?" He put out a finger and stroked her fur. I wanted to pull his hand away because I wanted to be the first to touch her. I know that puppies get to know you by your smell. I was trying not to be selfish. She lifted her head. Willie kept petting, but she looked right at me.

Maybe love at first sight is supposed to be between people like Rhett and Scarlett in *Gone with the Wind,* but I know it was love at first sight between me and that puppy.

I picked her up. First she whimpered a little, then stared at me. Her eyes were black and wet and shiny. She hardly weighed anything. I could feel her tiny bones right through the silky fur. I held her close. Her whole body was shaking. Scared. It was amazing. I could feel her heart pounding right next to mine. I could hardly tell where hers left off and mine began.

"Shh, darling," I said. "I'm going to take care of you. Don't worry. Don't be afraid. I love you." She closed her eyes. I could feel her sharp paws on my arms.

"The vet'll clip her toenails," said Norman. "She's six weeks old and, like I told ya on the phone, mostly beagle. At least her mother was. We don't know who her father was."

"How come no one knows who her father was? How can you not know who your father is?" I could have bet Willie would ask that.

"Who cares," I said. "She has a new family now. Open the door for me, Willie."

Norman walked over to us and gave the puppy a pat on the head. "Take good care of her, now. Don't let her wind up like those dogs back there." He nodded over his shoulder toward the back door. I guess he really did love animals. "Now go on, get outa here. I got work to do. For Pete's sake, two dollars and twenty-five cents."

"Well, now, isn't she a fine-looking girl?" said Mrs. Mac when we got outside.

"Oh, she's gorgeous, isn't she?" I asked. "Isn't she the most beautiful thing you ever saw?"

"Let me hold her now," said Willie.

"Why don't you wait until we get her home?" said Mrs. Mac. "Then she'll have time to get used to all of us."

The puppy was still trembling, and I watched carefully for bumps in the sidewalk. I wanted to give her a smooth walk home so she wouldn't be so scared.

"What are you going to call her?" asked Mrs. Mac.

Wasn't it funny? All the time I had wanted a puppy, I had never thought about names. I had just been too busy thinking about puppies.

"She's black and white; let's call her Spot," said Willie.

"That's dumb. Every dog in the world is called Spot," I said.

"Well, since we're keeping her a secret for a while, maybe we should think of something that describes that," said Mrs. Mac.

"Yeah, having her is a big secret," said Willie.

"We can't call her Secret," I said.

"No," agreed Mrs. Mac, "but when you finally tell your mother and father, this whole business of getting the dog and keeping it at my house will be like a mystery story."

Willie tried that out. "Mystery. Here, Mystery! No, I don't think that's a good name."

"Mystery." I said it quietly in her ear. "Mystery, my little Mystery." Her body wasn't shaking anymore, but her heart was still pounding. Her eyes were still so wet and worried-looking — kind of hazy, like there was a mist over them.

"Mist, my little Mist. No, Misty, little Misty."

"Misty," said Willie. "I like Spot better."

"Misty," said Mrs. Mac. "That sounds right. A pretty name for a pretty pup."

Whether or not we all fully agreed, Misty was her name by the time we reached the steps of her new temporary home.

six

Mrs. Mac opened her front door. "Just remember, I always leave it unlocked," she told us. "Bring Misty right in here."

We went into the room she called her parlor. The one with all the plants. This time I noticed a couple of old soft chairs. In the corner was a small cardboard box. There was a pile of newspapers next to it.

"Now, Willie, you start tearing the newspaper into strips to put into the box," said Mrs. Mac.

Misty had her eyes open, and she seemed to be looking around. But she didn't seem too anxious to get down on the floor. There was an old blanket next to the box and an alarm clock.

"Put her down," Mrs. Mac said, "and let's get her bed ready."

Boy, I thought I was so terrific in organizing everything. All I had thought about was getting the dog. I hadn't remembered about all the things we would need to take care of her — like a bed. I helped Willie rip newspapers. Misty slipped a little on the linoleum, but she seemed to want to stay close to me.

"Puppies tell everything by smell. See, Kim, she's used to you already."

"I want her to get used to me, too," cried Willie.

"Don't worry, Willie, she'll get to know everybody who loves her," said Mrs. Mac.

We put the blanket in the corner of the box, and then Mrs. Mac wound the alarm clock. "What's that for?" I asked.

"So when she sleeps tonight, she won't be lonely. She'll think it's a heart beating." I thought of how I had felt her heart against mine and hoped she would think the alarm clock was my heart.

Mrs. Mac had an old bowl that she filled with water. "Puppies need to drink lots," she said.

"Food," I yelled. "I forgot about food."

"On the kitchen table, straight through to your left."

"My goodness, Mrs. Mac, you thought of everything." She had, and I don't know why it hurt me. Maybe because she was so organized that Misty seemed like her puppy, not mine.

"Oh, I needed a roll for dinner, so I picked up the food when I went out this morning."

"Well, please put it on our bill." I was trying to make my voice sound official. After all, this was supposed to be a business deal.

"Oh, that's all right. I guess the old Social Security can stretch for one bag of puppy food."

"No, please, Mrs. Mac. Write down anything you lay out for Misty, and we'll pay it back."

"Very well, Kim." She showed us how to fill up the bowl with a little puppy food and mix it with water.

Misty went right to it. "Boy," said Willie. "I'll bet that Norman never feeds the dogs in there."

"You can't blame Norman," I said. "Don't forget, Misty just came from a family."

Mrs. Mac sat in a rocker that had a cushion

with pink roses on it. The stuffing was coming out of the edges. Willie and I sat on a scatter rug on the floor. All of us watched Misty. Her tiny red tongue flashed in and out like lightning. The bowl was empty before we knew it. Then she went to the bowl of water and drank some of that.

"I think she's still hungry," said Willie.

"No, that's enough for her," said Mrs. Mac. "It's better for her not to eat too much."

"Boy, it's lucky we found you, Mrs. Mac. You know everything about pups." Willie had on his big smile.

Mrs. Mac beamed one right back at him, and again I felt that sliver of hurt go through me. Mrs. Mac knew too darn much about puppies as far as I was concerned. Mom would probably say I was having one of my green-eyed monster jealousy attacks. But this was different from other things I was jealous over, like blond hair or being a great ballet dancer.

Mom! "Gee, Mrs. Mac, do you know what time it is?"

"My goodness," said Mrs. Mac, "it's five o'clock already."

"We've got to go." I stood up. "I have to heat up a casserole. Mom's probably home by now." I felt something tickling my ankles. It was Misty. She was curled up into a ball right on top of my shoes. I hadn't really thought what it would mean to leave her. But it was too late now.

"Look," said Willie. He pointed to a tiny trickle of yellow that was spreading on the newspaper around her box.

Mrs. Mac laughed. "Oh, you'll see plenty of that and worse, Willie, don't worry. We've got to paper-train her first before we get her to go outside."

I touched the back of her neck. She didn't move. Poor little thing, she was so tired out. Leaving her mother and her sisters and brothers, going to the pound and now here. I had read in my dog book that puppies cried at night. And I wouldn't be here. Probably by the time I got here tomorrow she would have forgotten all about me. After all, she had Mrs. Mac.

"Let's go." Willie was by the porch screen.

I stood up. Misty made a mewing sound and tried to cuddle up on my shoes again. Maybe I could sneak her into the house and upstairs to my room. Maybe she wouldn't cry and no one would know she was there. Maybe I could set the alarm for five o'clock in the morning and wake up before everyone else and bring her back here before school. Oh,

I knew I couldn't do any of those things. But I just couldn't leave her.

"What do you have on underneath that sweater, Kim?" asked Mrs. Mac.

Was she getting dippy? I was petting Misty. Couldn't she see I didn't want to go? Who cared what I had on underneath my sweater?

"Just a T-shirt," I said.

"Is it a good one?"

"No, it's old." Boy, how could I leave Misty with such a dippy old lady? "It's from last spring when we all went to Disney World."

"Then take it off and give it to me."

"What?"

"Well, we'll put it right in Misty's bed with the alarm clock, and then if she gets frightened during the night, she can smell your shirt and know that her new mother's coming tomorrow." Smell, of course! Why didn't I think of that?

I ducked into the living room to pull off the shirt. I put the sweater back on and buttoned it up to my neck. It was itchy without the T underneath, but we'd be going right home. I rolled the T-shirt into a ball and tucked it in the corner of the box. I lifted Misty and placed her right on it. She picked her head up and then, nose down, she sniffed twice and cuddled right into the shirt.

I felt a little better about leaving. Misty was in good hands until I could get back. Mrs. Mac sure knew a lot of things about puppies and people — probably because she was so old. I think it's information you get from just living a long time.

seven

We ran all the way, but the car was already in the driveway. Mom had beaten us home.

"Remember, Willie, don't mention Misty to Mommy or Daddy."

"Have I said one word yet?" He let out a big whoosh of air through his nose.

I had to admit that the old whiner really was keeping his mouth shut.

"But Kim, Miss Foster asked me when my mother is going to send in the PTA dues."

Uh-oh! "What did you tell her?"

"I just said Mommy was working and I'd bring the money in soon as she got paid."

Not only was he getting good at keeping his mouth shut, but he was becoming a great fibber. I knew there was some kind of law against corrupting minors — we had learned about it in social studies. I hoped I wasn't starting Willie on the road to crime.

I owed Mrs. Mac a dollar and a half for what she'd laid out for the food. I hadn't counted on that. But I'd really have to replace the PTA money before we got into trouble.

"Are we paying Mrs. Mac a lot of money, Kim?"

"No, not a lot of money. Why?"

"Well, I was thinking she could have some extras now, like Mommy says we can have since she's working."

"We're not paying Mrs. Mac the same kind of salary Mom gets, Willie."

"Oh. I thought with the money we pay her she won't have to worry about having a secretary every month."

"A secretary?" What was he talking about now?

"A secretary. Mrs. Mac keeps talking about her social secretary."

"That's Social *Security*, Willie. Money the government gives people to live on."

There were a couple of white hairs on his sweater. I picked them off. Leave it to Mom to notice something like that. Before I threw them away, I tried to smell them. They were too small. I couldn't smell Misty. I hoped my smell would stay in the T-shirt. I'd wear another one to bed under my pajamas so I could bring it to Mrs. Mac tomorrow. I'd have to keep refilling that smell so Misty wouldn't forget me. Maybe I shouldn't take a bath for a while. No, I don't think that's exactly the smell she'd like. I just wouldn't use any more strawberry bubblebath soap. I wouldn't want Misty to think her new mother was a berry patch.

Mom's shoes were in the living room near the couch where she had kicked them off. She never left shoes lying around before she started working. Now that's the first thing she does when she comes home. Off with her shoes. Her feet must really be killing her. She can't stand things to be sloppy and out of place.

She had the oven door open. "Hi, Kim." Her kiss landed someplace above my head, though I noticed that Willie's landed smack on his cheek. "What kind of adventure kept the two of you so busy today?"

"The park . . ." answered Willie.

"After-school play . . ." I said at the same time.

I raised my eyebrows and Willie caught on. He was learning to watch my face when we had conversations at home, which saved him a lot of black-and-blue marks from my pinches.

"Willie came with me to after-school play and then we went to the park."

"I'm really proud of both of you," said Mom. "Especially you, Kim. You're really taking on responsibility."

Mom was trying to give me a compliment, but she just made me feel squirmy.

"Hey, Mommy, if you think Kim is responsible, how about her dog?"

I tried to signal him again. He was too far away to pinch.

"What dog?" asked Mom.

"You know. The dog you promised her last summer."

"Oh, Willie, please. I thought we had that settled. No dog now. There's just too much going on for me to handle it."

I was able to breathe again. I'd thought for a minute that he was going to spill the beans. It was pretty funny. Mom thought I couldn't handle a future dog, and here I had one all stashed away already.

"What did you make tonight?" I pointed at the stove. I wanted to get away from dog talk.

"Tuna surprise," answered Mom.

She could do anything with tuna. Make it into salad, fry it into fish cakes, mix it with macaroni or spaghetti, and stuff it into tomatoes. It's lucky tuna was invented and lucky we liked it, because she had lots of trouble with things like chicken and roast beef.

I wondered if Misty would like tuna. In my dog books it said you weren't supposed to feed puppies table food. But I wanted her to eat as well as we did. I wondered if Mrs. Mac would remember to refill her water dish. Puppies had to have lots of water to drink.

"I've got homework, Mom."

"O.K., Kim, go upstairs and do it before dinner."

I shut my bedroom door and took out the book on dog care. I reread the chapter about bringing the puppy home. The book kept saying that the puppy would cry all night for its mother. And I wouldn't be there when Misty cried. I wondered where Mrs. Mac's bedroom was. We hadn't seen it. What if she didn't hear Misty cry? The very first night! I should be there. Really Misty should be here.

Mom was calling from the kitchen. "Dad's home. Supper, everybody!"

I threw the book against the wall. I don't know what she was so happy about. If she were home taking care of us like she was supposed to, then I could have Misty home and take care of her like *I* was supposed to.

The tuna surprise was a rice casserole with green and red pieces in it. They turned out to be pimentos and green pepper.

Mom was telling a story about her day. "And Mr. Dunbar had me checking references all day long." Mr. Dunbar was her boss. I wondered if I could sneak to the phone and call Mrs. Mac. If I had a phone in my room like Lisa, I could make a phone call in private.

"Why do you have to check references?" asked Willie.

"Well, when people come for a job, you ask if they've worked before or if someone knows them, like a former schoolteacher or a minister, and then you call and check on them."

"Why?" asked Willie.

"Because we have to know something about the people we hire. And I'm only an assistant personnel manager, so I get all the boring jobs to do that Mr. Dunbar thinks are beneath him."

I hoped Willie wouldn't catch that. I always tell him that he's my assistant when I want him to do something. Only I make him think an assistant is something really important.

"We never checked references for Mrs. you-know-who, Kim."

"References?" asked Daddy. "What would you have to check references for, Willie?"

"Willie." I let out a high giggle. "Hey, Willie, how come you're eating the rice, it's white."

"Kim," scolded Mom, "he was eating so nicely, why did you remind him?"

Willie studied his plate. "Well, I'm not eating anything that's all white, but this is O.K. because it has colors sprinkled in it."

"Besides," said Mom, "if you don't eat that, there's nothing else for supper."

Thank goodness he shut up while Mom served the chocolate pudding for dessert. "Is Nannie Marion on Social Security?" he asked.

Pudding is soft, but when you swallow a big glob, it makes an enormous lump in your chest.

"Are you studying Social Security in the first grade, Willie?" asked Daddy. The lump gave me a coughing fit, and by the time Mom brought me a glass of water and Daddy slapped me on the back, I think the subject of Social Security was forgotten. I wouldn't be able to let Willie out of my sight for a minute if this kept up.

"Help me clear, Bill, please," Mom said.

They did the dishes because I was responsible for Willie all day.

The phone rang. I answered it and heard Lisa. She thought she was whispering. You could have heard her in China.

"Did you get it?" she asked.

"Yeah." I looked over at the sink. Mom and Daddy were busy talking.

"What does the D-O-G look like?" I don't know why she spelled out *dog*. The only one in the house who couldn't spell was Willie, and he knew about the dog.

"I really can't talk now. I have to do my homework."

"O.K. Listen, Kim, I want to go with you tomorrow to see the D-O-G. O.K.?" She was driving me crazy with this spelling.

"Yeah, yeah, O.K., I'll see you tomorrow." I hung up. Then I realized that I had planned not to let her see Misty the first time she asked. I was just too good a person. I had forgotten completely about paying her back.

I had a hard time falling asleep. I kept thinking of Misty. She was so tiny, about the size of a small loaf of bread. Her hair was so silky. I wondered if I could put a bow in it like they do on poodles. She didn't have any brown hair like beagles do. They're black, brown, and white. She was just black and white. I wondered what kind of dog her father was. I decided not to try ribbons. She was pretty enough the way she was. She didn't need fancy things.

I guess I fell asleep, because the next thing I heard were the hair blowers going early in the morning. Both Mom and Daddy fought over who was going to be first in the bathroom. I put my head under the pillow for another five-minute snooze when I remembered. Misty! Here I had thought I'd never fall asleep, and it was morning already. I pulled on a pair of jeans and a T-shirt and ran into Willie's room. I yanked his toes. "Come on, Willie," I whispered.

"Leave me alone," he said. He tried to crawl back under the covers. "I'm going to tell Mommy. It's too early to get up."

I grabbed the blanket hard at the foot of the bed. It landed on the floor.

"Willie." I pinched his ear. "Misty. Remember? We wanted to pass Mrs. Mac's and see Misty before school."

It was quicker than dropping ice cubes down his neck. He was out of bed and had his pajama top off before I was even out of the room.

"What's the rush this morning?" asked Mom as I got ready to leave.

"Oh, I promised Mrs. Brock I'd help water the plants today, and she said Willie could stay with me until the bell rang." I crossed my fingers as I said this. It was almost true. I was in charge of the plants this month, except I watered them during first period, not before school.

We got to Mrs. Mac's out of breath. "Jogging's good for you, Willie. You'll be in great condition for sports. Maybe you'll be a professional when you grow up."

"I don't want to be in sports when I grow up. I want to own a supermarket."

Just when I think I understand this kid, I don't. Every other little boy I know wants to be an astronaut or a fireman or a cowboy. My brother wants a grocery store. And he doesn't even like food!

We walked right into the house, like Mrs. Mac told us to. I didn't think it was very safe for her to leave the door open like that. Maybe she didn't read about all the burglars and muggers that were around. Though a burglar would probably pass by her house because it looked so run-down. Unless she turned out to be one of those crazy old ladies that have loads of money stashed away in their mattresses.

"Mrs. Mac," I called out.

I heard barking. Boy, she was loud. Her lungs must be great for such a tiny pup.

"We're in the sun parlor. Come right in."

And there she was. My little Misty. She was running across the room. Away from us.

"Hi, Misty," yelled Willie.

"Not so loud," I said, "you'll scare her."

I think she was scared for a few minutes, because she stood looking at us. Her nose was quivering. I could see the little whiskers shaking. Her eyes looked very watery, as if she were crying. She walked closer to Mrs. Mac. I knew she would forget me overnight. But no, she put her nose down and sniffed around the floor. We waited as she sniffed her way across the room. She sniffed Willies shoes and mine. I didn't think she'd recognize me from my sneakers. They're pretty old and pretty stinky. I wouldn't want her to think I smelled like my sneakers. She must have remembered something about us, because she jumped and ran between our legs as if she wanted to play.

I bent to pick her up, and she snuggled in my arms and reached up to lick my face.

"Did she cry last night?" I asked.

"Let me hold her. Let me hold her." I didn't want to let go, but Willie looked so eager, I had to.

"Be gentle," I said. "Did she eat breakfast, Mrs. Mac? Can we feed her?" I saw a pile of newspapers in the corner. "Oh, did she wet all over? Should we take her outside? How can we get her trained?"

"Slow down," said Mrs. Mac. "She was very good. Cried a little, but that's to be expected. We watched the late show together. She sat right in my lap over there." Mrs. Mac pointed to the rocker with the pink roses on the cushion. "I gave her some puppy food this morning, and we watched the Good Morning show on TV." I hoped that Misty wasn't too close to the TV set. I thought maybe I'd better tell Mrs. Mac about radiation from sitting close. I wasn't sure if all that watching was good for a dog's eyes.

I took Misty back in my arms and rubbed my chin across the top of her head. She felt like the velvety bathrobe that Mom wore when we had company for breakfast.

"Willie, grab that pile of newspapers and throw them outside for me."

"I'll do it," I said and put Misty down. She sniffed around and found an edge of paper, and before I realized what was going to happen, there was a yellow trickle spreading across the floor.

"She better get trained quick," said Willie. "Mom'll kill us if she wets on our carpeting."

"Takes time to train pups, just like children," said Mrs. Mac. She wasn't wearing an apron today. She had on an old pair of army pants and a heavy sweater.

"You kids better hurry off for school. You'll be late."

"What are you and Misty going to do this morning?" I wiped up the trickle with a rag Mrs. Mac gave me.

"Just pour a little vinegar on that rag," she said, handing me the bottle. "It helps take the smell away. Puppies always make where they've made before. That's why they sniff around like that. So you've got to wipe up carefully and put fresh paper down."

Misty had curled up in her box. She looked like she was going to take a nap.

Mrs. Mac kept talking. "I have to dig up some tulip bulbs from my garden this morning." I looked out the window. I didn't see much garden, just lots of grass that needed cutting and some dried-up flowers.

"Then, this afternoon, Misty's going with me to the Senior Center to play bingo."

"Bingo?"

"Yep. Tuesday is bingo day. I never miss it. Me and Mrs. Johnson and Mrs. Goldberg from up the block have been going to the bingo on Tuesdays for about twenty years."

"How are you going to take Misty?" Willie asked before I could.

"No problem," she said. "I'll feed her lunch before we go, and I made a carrying case for her." She showed us an old leather pocketbook with a soft lining. The top had been cut off. She picked up Misty and plunked her inside. Misty curled right up.

"She fits right in and can have a nice nap at the center."

I wished I could pick up that old pocketbook and let Misty have a nice nap while I was in school. Maybe I could leave her in my locker. No, that wouldn't be any good. She wouldn't get enough air.

"Misty and I will be back before you and Willie come from school, so run along. You do your work and I'll do mine. Remember, you hired me to be a dog-sitter."

I remembered, but now I wasn't so sure. I

took out six dollars and fifty cents from my pocket. "Here, Mrs. Mac, I know you had to lay out money for the food, and here's some advance for your salary." That left me with one dollar for an emergency, and I knew we still had to take Misty to a veterinarian. Maybe I could find one that would let me pay on the installment plan.

I hugged Misty once more. Her paws were so tiny and that little tongue was so cute the way it flicked in and out. Her whole body felt so delicious you could squeeze it to pieces.

Willie and I left for school. A puppy going to bingo? I never read anything like that in my dog-care books.

eight

M rs. Brock called me up to her desk during study period. "Is anything wrong, Kim?" she asked.

"No, nothing, Mrs. Brock."

"I just wondered. You were so excited about the advanced reading program, and you haven't handed in any extra reports."

Extra reports! I knew she was trying to be nice, but if Mrs. Brock knew all the things on my mind, she wouldn't be bugging me about any extra reading reports.

"I understand your mother went back to work."

Uh-oh. Here it comes. She had her "Tell - me - your - troubles - and - I'll - help - you -

make - them - go - away" voice. Next thing you know she'd be calling the school psychologist. Gee whiz, if you didn't walk around giggling and happy or you acted a little different from usual in this school, everyone thought you needed a little talk.

"My mother goes to work, but that O.K."

"Does that mean you have a lot to do at home?"

"No, I just have to watch my little brother."

"Isn't that too much responsibility for you?"

"No, I like to do it. Besides, I get paid."

"It's just that I'd like to see you take advantage of the extra reading."

"I'll try, Mrs. Brock."

Lisa punched me in the back when I returned to my seat. "What did she want?"

"Extra reading," I whispered.

Amy sent a note through me to Lisa. "You can read it, too, Kim" was written on the front. I opened it up. "REMEMBER — DISCO dancing — this FRIDAY — What should we wear???? Pass it on." I did. What did I care what they wore to disco dancing? I would be busy with Misty.

I did ask Lisa if she was going with me that afternoon.

"Of course, dummy!"

Well, I had to be sure. Lisa was like one of those desert chameleons we'd studied about. They change their color when they're in different surroundings. Lisa changed her personality depending on who she was with. She would be acting like the old Lisa, giggling with me and having fun, and then Doug or one of the other boys would go by and she would change into an imitation of some actress she saw in a TV movie.

She kept her word, though. Willie and I waited while she had two conversations with Amy, ran to the drinking fountain so she could go past Doug and Mark, and went to the john to comb her hair in case she met somebody while we were walking down the street.

"Who's she going to meet?" asked Willie. "Doesn't she want to see Misty? Mrs. Mac won't care if her hair is combed."

"You don't understand girls, Willie," I said.

"You're a girl," he answered. "I understand you." Oh, that was great. I figured I'd never be like Lisa and Amy and the others if even my brother could understand me.

Finally she was ready, and we raced each other to Mrs. Mac's. Lisa won. Changing into a girl who combed her hair all the time hadn't affected her feet. She always beat me when we raced.

The door was open as usual. We went in and Lisa looked around. "Boy," she said. "This place looks like it's going to fall down any minute."

"You think so?" asked Willie.

"Oh, don't be silly," I said. "It's been standing for fifty years, it'll last another fifty. Now, don't start scaring Willie, Lisa."

Still, I had noticed the broken steps on our first visit. I looked up. There were lots of shingles missing from the roof, and the house sort of tilted to one side.

"We're in the parlor," called out Mrs. Mac.

"The parlor?" asked Lisa.

"That's like a living room," Willie said. "You know, like in the olden days."

"That linoleum has holes in it and you can see the radiator pipes," whispered Lisa. I was used to the house already, but I could see how shabby Lisa would think it was. "And look at that lamp."

It was tilted the same as the house, with a wooden base and a big ruffled lampshade over it. Some of the ruffles were shredding and the strings were hanging loose.

"Here you are." There was Mrs. Mac, holding Misty.

Lisa forgot about the linoleum and radiator pipes. "Oh, she's adorable. Let me hold her, let me hold her."

I introduced everybody. Misty barked and sniffed at Lisa, but she finally let her hold her. Then Willie wanted a chance, and finally I got her.

Mrs. Mac had a plate of donuts on the table and a container of milk. She had three glasses out and napkins folded into triangles. "How about some refreshments?" She brought out another glass for Lisa.

I felt funny because I knew what a tight budget she was on. She shouldn't be spending any of her money on donuts for us kids.

Mrs. Mac picked one up and took a big bite. Some of the powdered sugar stuck to her thumb and she licked it off. "Mmm, good. They served them at bingo. There were a lot left over, so we all divided them up."

I felt better about that. I could eat one with a clear conscience. While Lisa and Willie got busy with the milk and donuts, I walked into the front room with Misty. I could feel her heart, but it was much calmer today. I rested my chin on the top of her head. I was afraid to squeeze too hard. She reached up and licked my cheek. I hadn't noticed her doing that to anyone else.

"Thank goodness you remember me." She licked again as if to answer me. I loved her ears — they were so soft. Once I had pulled the petals off a dark red American beauty rose. The inside petals had felt just like Misty's ears.

"I have so much to tell you, Misty, and we can't even be alone yet." I looked at her face carefully. My dog book told me that the eyes and nose should be clear. She looked fine to me.

There were a couple of old tables in the room with pictures on them. I walked around and showed them to Misty, hugging and rubbing her all the time. She felt so good and cuddly. I remember when my Aunt Jen had her baby. She used to bury her nose in his neck and say, "Oh, I could just eat you up." Willie and I used to laugh, but I now felt the same way about Misty. I whispered all kinds of silly things to her. At least I knew she would keep my secrets and understand them. She nipped at the string around my wrist. I bet I could put a string around her paw and she would keep it for me.

Mrs. Mac called, "Hate to interrupt you, Kim, but we have business to attend to."

She handed me a slip of paper with an address and the words "Dr. Lyons, 3:45, Thursday."

"I asked around today at bingo and found out about Dr. Lyons. He's retired from full-time practice but he still has hours once a week. He'll see Misty for you."

"Remember, Norman told us she had to go right to the vet," said Willie.

"Of course, I know that. Is he very expensive?"

Lisa was still chewing a donut. "Eddie Feeny's dog is a pedigree, and his mother tells my mother that the doctor bills are stupendous. He needs special foods and shots. He has a delicate stomach."

"Who, Eddie?" asked Willie.

"No, silly. Eddie's no pedigree. It's his dog."

"Well, I think Misty looks very healthy. I asked Dr. Lyons and he said he'd examine Misty and give her a shot for five dollars. That's a bargain." Mrs. Mac offered me a donut. It might be a bargain, but to me it was another five dollars. I'd just have to juggle things around some more. I put Misty's food in her dish and we all watched her eat. Then Willie and I cleaned out her box and put fresh newspaper strips in it. We also placed newspaper in the corner we were trying to train her to use. It was time to leave. She was curled up in Mrs. Mac's lap on the rocking chair. The TV was on. She looked up once as we walked out. Then she curled back up into a ball no bigger than a hank of knitting wool.

We ran home. I didn't want to be late too many days in a row, or Mom would start to get suspicious. I figured I better ask Daddy to advance me more baby-sitting money. I hadn't repaid the PTA dues yet. I planned to write everything down to keep it straight when I got home.

"Don't forget," said Lisa as we got to her house. "Disco dancing Friday."

"Oh, I won't." That was it! Disco dancing! I'd ask for the ten dollars for disco dancing. Then I'd use five dollars for the vet and put five down on the dancing and pay that off and the PTA dues when I got all my money.

It worked pretty well, too. Mom had a headache when she came home, so she just handed me the ten dollars without a word when I said I needed it for disco dancing. As a matter of fact, she didn't look too good. She couldn't finish eating and decided to go upstairs and take a nap.

"Don't you think working is too much for her?" I asked Daddy.

"Maybe she needs vitamins like those ladies on TV," said Willie.

"No, it's not the work, kids," said Daddy. "It's just that her boss is giving her a hard time, and she's got to decide for herself what to do about it."

That was something to think about. I never thought anybody could give Mom a hard time. One time a TV repairman came and put in a new picture tube and charged us fifty dollars. Mom called up his boss and told him we were under a guarantee and she didn't care if he came and took the set away, she wasn't going to pay.

"Why can't she just tell her boss that she doesn't like the way he's treating her?" Willie asked.

Daddy laughed. "It doesn't work that way in the real world, Willie. Sometimes you have to decide what things you're going to swallow and what you're not going to allow."

"So Mommy's sick because she swallowed something?" Willie asked.

I giggled.

"It's not funny, Kim," said Daddy. "What I mean, Willie, is that sometimes people upset their whole bodies because they're holding back from telling things they're not sure they're ready to say."

"Does everybody get sick when they hold back telling?"

"Willie." I stood up and handed him a plate. I used my sweetest big-sister voice. "Let's help Mom by stacking the dishes in the dishwasher." All I needed was for him to think he was getting sick because he was keeping a secret.

nine

I was a little nervous about going to the vet. I'm brave about most things, but doctors scare me.

"Are you going with us, Mrs. Mac?" I asked.

"Oh, I'm sorry, Kim." She was wearing a plastic apron and her feet were bare. She had a big watering can, a little brass one with a long nozzle, and a pair of scissors.

"I've got to get after some of these plants. Mr. Brady is in Florida and his coleus has a lot of dead leaves. I wouldn't be doing my job if he comes home to a drooping plant, now, would I?"

Dr. Lyons's office was in a little brick attachment on the side of his house. We went inside. There was a lady with a covered birdcage on one of the waiting-room benches.

"Now, children, you keep that dirty dog away from my Brenda, you hear?" She shook her finger at us.

I was carrying Misty. "She's not dirty," said Willie.

"Shh," I told him, "don't answer back."

"Well, she's not dirty."

We sat down on a bench. The lady held her cage closer. "I have to keep it covered. Brenda is very sensitive to the light. And she's frightened when she leaves home. As a matter of fact, I don't like to go out much myself."

We didn't answer.

She continued. "I would show you Brenda, but she doesn't like strangers, especially children!" She said "children" as if we were creatures from an unidentified flying object.

Willie sat quietly. Misty had started shaking the minute we walked through the door. I tried to pet her, but she was trembling all over. Maybe she could smell that it was a doctor's office. Whenever I go for my yearly checkup, I can smell doctor the minute I walk into the office.

A door opened. "Well, if it isn't Brenda and Miss Tressingham. Why don't you come right in." He turned to us. "I'll be right with you, children."

She stood up. "I just don't know what to do with Brenda, Doctor. She won't eat a thing, even when I put the seeds through the grinder twice."

"That's probably the trouble, Miss Tressingham. You're making it too easy for her."

I couldn't hear her answer because they went into the examining room, but I did hear a little squawk from the cage, so maybe Brenda was trying to get her two cents in.

"He looked nice, didn't he?" asked Willie.

I thought so, too, in the quick look I had gotten. He had on a white coat and he had nice white hair and a little mustache. There were lots of diplomas on the walls. I picked up Misty and walked around and read them. He certainly had gone to a lot of schools to be a veterinarian.

The door opened. Miss Tressingham came out hugging the birdcage. "Well, I hope you're right, Dr. Lyons."

"Brenda will be fine, Miss Tressingham. Remember, lots of sun and air. That goes for you, too."

She sort of sniffed at the air as she left the office. He held the door open. "O.K., in you go and let's take a look at the pup." He reached for Misty. She was shaking, so I cuddled her closer. Maybe she was afraid of the metal table in the examining room and all those bottles and things that were lying around. Maybe he was a mad scientist who would use Misty for an experiment. After all, I was only in sixth grade, how was I supposed to know everything?

"Come on, Kim," said Willie, "Dr. Lyons is waiting. You're prostinating."

"Procrastinating," I corrected him, which proved my mind was still working.

"Yeah, procrasin, whatever that word is that Mommy always says you do."

I guess when it comes to doctors I would just have to trust Willie's judgment. He had the most experience with them. I handed her over.

Dr. Lyons *was* really nice, and the examination went very quickly. He checked Misty's eyes and nose and felt all over her body for lumps. He even took her temperature. "Everything seems fine, children."

I breathed a sigh of relief. Willie and I were holding Misty to keep her quiet on the metal table.

"Now she just gets her shot. She needs two more for full immunization."

Dr. Lyons got a hypodermic needle ready. He squirted some water in the air to test it. Needles make my knees feel weak. I didn't think I could look. But I didn't want to desert Misty.

"Don't worry," said Willie. "I'm used to needles. I can hold her." He put both arms around Misty. I turned my back to the table and covered my eyes. "Tell me when it's over."

Before I knew it, Dr. Lyons said, "O.K., Misty. You can turn around now, Kim, it's all over."

She hadn't even let out a peep. I put my arms around her and hugged.

"All set," said Dr. Lyons. "Just stop by as soon as you can and leave me a specimen of her bowel movements."

"What's that for?" asked Willie.

"I have to test for worms. Many small puppies have worms."

Worms! My knees were shaking again. There certainly was a lot to taking care of a puppy.

I gave Dr. Lyons five dollars, and he gave me a receipt to take to the town hall. "What's this for?" I asked.

"Her license, Kim. It costs twelve dollars, and you have to bring proof that she's been inoculated."

Twelve dollars! I couldn't believe it. If I didn't get at my bank account soon, Willie and I would be wiped out.

The doctor must have seen my face, because he said, "You have four weeks to register her."

That was a little better. Four weeks to get another twelve dollars. At least I had a little time to think. We walked back to Mrs. Mac's house, taking turns carrying Misty.

"Hey, Kim, we should really get her a collar and a leash."

"I know, but right now we're dead broke." Poor Misty. I stroked her back. Maybe a rich family would have come in to adopt her. Instead she got stuck with me. She was entitled to a little luxury like a nice leather dog collar. I'd price them at the pet store and see just how much they were. Maybe I could get a loan from one of those places that advertise on TV where they give you one lump sum of money to pay off all your debts, and then you just pay back the finance company in one easy payment a month. But I didn't think they'd be interested in advancing money to an eleven-and-a-half-year-old girl with a six-week-old puppy.

Mrs. Mac had finished with the plants, and her kitchen smelled delicious.

Willie sniffed. "Mmm, what's that?" We put Misty down on the floor, and she ran right over to Mrs. Mac. Mrs. Mac sat in her rocker and plopped Misty on her lap. Misty curled up tighter and tighter, and after a couple of rocks we could tell she was sound asleep.

"After my watering I had a special job to do for Ms. Gold. She's having company tomorrow, and I made three big noodle puddings for her and some chicken salad. She buys the ingredients, and I just charge a small sum for making the dishes."

That was an idea. Mrs. Mac certainly had all different ways of making money. Maybe I could bake something and sell it. I couldn't think of anything special that I made except macaroni and cheese, and anybody can make that. I also bake chocolate-chip cookies, but I use a mix.

Mrs. Mac leaned her head back against the rocker. Her hand smoothed Misty's fur. "My daughter called today. You know, Charlene, from Ohio? She's after me again to come out and live with her. Tells me I'm too old to be living here alone. That I can't make ends meet. She'd really throw a fit if she saw what came today."

Mrs. Mac pointed to a piece of paper on the table. I picked it up and read it. I didn't understand all of it, but it was from the tax office and said something about taxes overdue.

"They raised the taxes again on this old house. I barely scraped through last year. Don't see how I'll do it again this year."

"But you have money from taking care of Misty and cooking and watering plants." Willie walked to the side of the rocker.

"That and my Social Security just about pays my expenses, Willie. But I need three hundred dollars in cash for the tax bill."

Three hundred dollars! And here I was worrying about twelve. I should really be thinking of a way to help Mrs. Mac.

"Will they throw you out of here if you don't pay?" Willie asked.

"Now, don't you worry. They don't throw old ladies out on the street anymore." She winked at me. "It's bad publicity. I can hold out — as long as I can keep Charlene from finding out."

Well, she wouldn't hear it from Willie or me. It was time to leave. "Tomorrow I've got to stop at disco dancing, Mrs. Mac. Otherwise someone might tell my mother I didn't go there."

"That's all right, Kim, me and Misty will be fine."

That's what I was afraid of. If I didn't keep coming around, Misty and Mrs. Mac would get along perfectly well without me.

ten

Mom came home happy. She was humming and had a stack of papers under her arm. "I couldn't fit everything in my briefcase. Please help me, Kim."

"What is all this, Mom?"

"Homework. Just put it on my desk."

"Homework?" asked Willie.

"Right. I've decided that there's no sense in walking around complaining about Mr. Dunbar and the boring stuff I'm stuck with. By studying the company records, I found out they have an inefficient vacation policy, so I'm going to work on a completely new plan for a sensible vacation schedule. Mr. Dunbar said as long as I worked on my own time, he'd see that I get a chance to present it at the monthly management meeting." She and Willie went into the kitchen.

She sure had a stack of work. I tried to make a neat pile of the papers. I didn't like her being away from home every day, but I was kind of proud of her. She was really trying to make her job work. I followed them in.

"Hey, Mom, can I take some money out of my bank account?"

She turned away from the stove and looked at me. "What for, Kim? You get three dollars a week for taking care of Willie, and we pay all your expenses. What do you need money for?"

I looked at Willie. He was munching a carrot. "Nothing, Mom, I was just wondering whether I could take something out of the bank if I really desperately needed money."

She turned back to the stove. "If you're really desperate, see Daddy or me. The money in the bank is for college."

I went up to my room. Sure, see her — and tell her I needed money for a dog that I wasn't supposed to have. I started adding everything up on a piece of paper. Things didn't look too good. I was getting three dollars a week for taking care of Willie. but I was paying Mrs. Mac six dollars a week. That wasn't very smart. I already owed four dollars for PTA dues and a dollar and a half to Lisa, and I had taken five dollars of the disco money for Misty's shot.

I had six dollars left, five dollars of which I had to give for disco tomorrow. I drew big black Xs on the paper and lay down across my bed and shut my eyes. What would Mom do in my place? Think up another plan, that's what.

I started with Daddy at supper. "Daddy, I think I'm entitled to more than three dollars a week for taking care of Willie."

"Oh, you do, do you? What makes you think so?"

I knew he'd say something like that.

"Well . . . because some of the other kids in school get three dollars a week allowance without doing anything."

Mother waved her fork in the air. "You know we're not interested in what other families do, Kim."

"Well, I think I'm worth double the money. Six dollars a week at least."

Willie picked out the tomatoes from his salad. He was off red now. "I think so, too, Daddy. I'm hard to take care of."

"Willie," Mom interrupted. "You're going to miss a lot of good food by not eating red."

"What good food, tomatoes and beets? Ech!" He made a face.

"What about strawberry jam or cherries or watermelon?" Mom said.

"What about the raise in my salary?" I said.

Daddy wiped his chin. "Maybe you're right, Kim." He looked over at Mom. She shook her head back. "How about if we compromise? We'll give you a dollar a day. That's five dollars a week."

Whew! I let out a breath, jumped up, and ran over to kiss him. "Oh, thanks, Daddy, you're the greatest. You're the greatest too, Mom."

"Pretty good, Kim." She smiled. "You just earned yourself a two-dollar raise through negotiation. We'll have to watch out for you."

Before I went to bed, I opened my window and looked out over the houses toward Mrs. Mac's. "Good night, Misty," I said. It was silly. She couldn't hear me. "It's not time to bring you home, but maybe soon."

I felt like killing someone when I got to school the next day. I had on the corduroy jumper that I had let Mom buy because Lisa had said all the girls were going to wear skirts. Everyone had on jeans and T-shirts except for Myra Harkevy, and she just transferred from a private school and always wore plaid skirts with blazer jackets.

"Why didn't you tell me, Lisa?" I slammed my locker shut.

"Tell you what?" She had rigged up a mirror on the top shelf of her locker. She had on blue eye shadow and mascara. I'll bet her mother didn't know.

"You have black smeared under your eyes."

"Oh, darn." She reached for a tissue and just made it worse. Good, let her feel like a jerk for once.

"That everyone was going to wear jeans."

"Oh." She looked over at me. "We just decided late last night. That's O.K., you look really cute in the jumper."

Cute! Chimpanzees in the zoo were cute, too. I twirled the string around my wrist. It was getting more and more frayed, but it still hadn't fallen off.

I gave my five dollars to Mrs. Brock. "Can I bring the other five in next week?"

"I guess so, Kim." I thought she looked at me a little strangely, but maybe that's what happens when you walk around with a guilty conscience. What a waste of perfectly good money anyway.

Mrs. Brock yelled at the class five times during the day. They were so excited, it seemed as if they couldn't shut up or stay in their seats.

"If I have to call this class to order once more, there won't be any disco dancing."

Good, I thought. I hope she sticks to it. But I knew she wouldn't. Besides, once the PTA decided to do something good for the students, nothing could stop it.

Finally the bell. Everyone ran for the gym except for those girls who ran for the bathroom to comb their hair. I noticed that Myra Harkevy now had on jeans. She must have gone home at lunch to change. So I was the only girl with a skirt. I looked like I was going to the queen's inauguration or something!

Music was blaring from the gym. Even though I didn't want them to, my feet started tapping in spite of myself. Maybe it wouldn't be too bad. There was the instructor, Mr. Simmons, dancing by himself and going "chucka, chucka, chucka" in time to the music. Some of the PTA mothers had taken lessons from him, and that's how he got hired to teach the sixth grade. He had on a silk shirt that was open to the waist and lots of gold chains that jangled around his neck. He was a pretty good dancer, though.

The boys were on one side of the gym in a big group. I joined the girls on the opposite side.

"O.K., fellas and gals, everyone grab a partner." He clapped his hands. Nobody moved for a moment; we just stared at him. Then the boys re-formed into a big huddle and so did the girls.

There were a couple of PTA mothers setting up a table with lemonade and cookies. Some boys were trying to sneak over for refreshments, but the mothers were firm. "No dancing, no refreshments."

Mr. Chucka Chucka tried again. This time he snapped his fingers. "Let's grab a partner, fellas. Time to learn the hustle!"

Oh, brother! Doug grabbed Scott and snapped his own fingers. "Hey, Scott, will you be my partner? Hey, Mr. Simmons, I've got a partner." He was trying to imitate a giggling girl. The other boys were big copycats. They grabbed each other and ran back and forth across the gym as if they were dancing. I was next to Lisa. Amy was practically crying. "This is terrible. I'm going to tell my mother. We paid ten dollars for this, and the boys won't even dance."

Mr. Chucka Chucka was trying to get the boys back in line. "Come on, fellas," he was pleading. I folded my arms across my chest. I'd known it was going to turn out like this. The same thing happened when we had to square-dance in gym — only the gym teacher wouldn't stand for it. He had blown his whistle, made us count off by twos, and had us in partners before anyone could get away.

Someone turned the speed up on the record player so that the music sounded real screechy and the singers sounded like Mickey Mouse. I got a laugh at that, except I was worried about Willie. He was supposed to walk over to Mrs. Mac's by himself. It was only two blocks, and he knew the way. Other little kids walked by themselves. Still, I was responsible for him.

Finally Mr. Simmons turned the music off completely. He wiped his brow. He was sweating, and he hadn't even begun teaching us. I hadn't noticed before, but he wore a toupée that was slipping backward. A few more chucka-chucka turns and it might come off altogether. "O.K.," he said, "I thought we could be friends, but if this is the way you want to be . . ."

I was glad to see he was getting smarter. He could be our friend or our teacher, but he couldn't be both.

He passed out a card from a full deck to each boy, then from another deck to the girls. He called out combinations. "Will the fella who has the queen of hearts and the gal who has the queen of hearts come out? You are a couple."

It was Amy and Scott. Scott threw his card on the floor and made believe he was choking. "No, no, anything but that! I give up. Kill me, but I won't dance." He tried to change cards with Doug, but Mr. Simmons made him come out on the floor. My heart was beating. I'd die if someone didn't want to dance with me and made a big fuss.

He began calling the cards out more quickly. We had already used up half the dancing time. He called the eight of spades. That was me. Whew! The other eight of spades was Eddie Feeny. We stood together waiting for the rest of the kids to be picked. I didn't know what to say, and I guess Eddie didn't either, so neither of us said a word. I was trying to think of something, and then I remembered his dog.

"Hey, Eddie, how's your dog?"

"Yeah, O.K. Pretty good. The only thing,

he was in a show last week and got eliminated."

"Why?"

"Well, it was for pedigrees, and his ears aren't perfect. They don't stand up straight."

I couldn't believe it. "For a little thing like that, he got eliminated?"

"Yeah, well, show dogs have to be perfect."

Boy, I was glad Misty wasn't a pedigree. I felt my own ears. I'd probably be thrown out of the show, too. My ears stuck out a mile, but I always tried to cover them with my hair.

Mr. Simmons began to teach us. It wasn't bad. After everybody shut up, it was kind of fun to learn. The time went quickly, and the mothers began to pour the lemonade. I told Eddie I had to go. "Aren't you even going to have a cookie?"

Quickly I told him about Misty and how I had to get over there to pick up Willie.

"Mostly beagle, huh? Must be a really cute dog. Maybe I'll go over with you and see her."

Before I knew it, Eddie and I were both on our way to Mrs. Mac's house. She didn't even act surprised to see me with a stranger. Misty left Willie and ran right over to me, though she stopped when she saw Eddie and barked a lot. We had lots of fun. We took

Misty out in the yard, and she chased us back and forth. I got her dinner ready, and then it was time to leave.

"Mrs. Mac says we have to give her a bath next week," said Willie.

"A bath?"

"That's fun. Can I come and help you?" Eddie was roughing up the fur around her ears. "Our dog is so delicate, he has to get groomed in a special dog beauty parlor, so I never get a chance to wash him."

"Sure," said Mrs. Mac. Then she stopped. "Well, it's not for me to say, it's really up to Kim. After all, Misty is her dog."

"Sure," I said. "That would be great, Eddie. I never bathed a dog before."

"Then it's all settled," said Mrs. Mac as we said goodbye. "Misty's first bath is next week."

I was happy on the way home, and after we left Eddie at his house, I said "chucka, chucka" to myself all the way home.

eleven

I didn't expect Lisa's call, or Amy's, or Ellen's. They must have rehearsed, because they were sweet as sugar and said the same things. Next week, they told me, all of us girls were going to wear skirts to disco dancing. Then they asked where Eddie and I had gone. I don't know what the big deal was. Lisa acted as if I was trying to out-traitor Benedict Arnold. "You didn't even tell me, Kim! And we're supposed to be best friends."

Ha! Best friends whenever it suited her. "Eddie and I just went to see Misty."

"You should have told me. You know how I love Misty. Remember, I was the one who helped you find Mrs. Mac. And I gave you my lip-gloss money and everything."

That was true. Lisa always knew how to soften me up. "So next week, if you and Eddie go, tell me. Maybe Eddie can talk to Doug and he can go, too."

That was it. She wanted to use Misty as an excuse to be with Doug.

Willie and I had lots of free time to go back and forth to Mrs. Mac's because Mom brought home more work for the weekend. Late Saturday afternoon she was going through the mail when she called us. "Kim, Willie, do you know what this is all about?"

It was a note from the PTA. My cheeks got very hot and my stomach dropped. The note was very polite. It was a reminder to Mom to please send in her PTA dues. Mom had her hair tied back with a rubber band, and she scratched under the ponytail with her pen. "I can't understand it. I looked in my checkbook and I can't find a stub made out to the PTA. But I was sure I left you cash. Do either of you remember?"

We didn't answer. Mom was leafing through the papers on her desk. "Of course, with all the excitement of my working, maybe I forgot." I squeezed Willie's hand. He didn't say a word.

110

It's for you, Misty. It's for you, I kept saying to myself. We weren't exactly lying. We just weren't answering Mom.

She kept talking, almost to herself. "I guess I must have forgotten. These last few weeks have been crazy." She wrote out a check and sealed it in an envelope. "Drop it in the mailbox on the corner when you go out again, will you, Kim? It's a little embarrassing to get dunned by the PTA."

"What's *dun* mean?" asked Willie.

"It's when you don't pay your bills. First you get polite notes, then they get a little tougher, and finally they tell you to pay up or else."

I took the envelope from her. I felt bad. I hadn't realized that the PTA would go after Mom for the money. I thought we could pay it back in time. She said people probably thought she was neglecting her responsibilities because of working full-time.

"Let's go to the mailbox, Willie." We walked to the corner.

"Can Mommy go to jail, Kim?"

"What are you talking about?"

"You know, for not paying PTA dues?"

"Don't be silly. She doesn't *have* to join the PTA."

"She'd be pretty mad at us if she knew we took the money, wouldn't she?"

"I guess so."

He started to sniffle. "I don't want Mommy to be mad at me, Kim."

"Oh, don't be stupid." I pulled his arm. "She wouldn't be made at you anyway. You're too little. She'd be mad at me." He was crying harder now. I remembered all the times he used to cry over nothing. That's when I had called him Willie the Whiner. But now I didn't blame him for crying. I tried to cheer him up.

"Besides, in a couple of weeks we'll be able to tell Mom and bring Misty home. Once she sees her, she'll fall in love with her and she won't be mad anymore."

"Do you really think so?"

I wasn't sure, but Willie's tears were making me feel very guilty. "Isn't Mom working on a plan to solve the problems at her plant? She'll realize that we were doing the same thing."

"Really?"

"Sure."

Willie wiped his nose with the back of his hand. I dropped the letter in the box. It was times like these that made me wish I was the younger child. It would be nice to have an older brother or sister to make things all better for me for a change.

Daddy took us to The Pancake House for Sunday brunch. I watched Willie carefully, but he ate a gigantic stack of buttermilk pancakes. Mom was so happy that his appetite was improving. I guess he must have believed me that everything would be all right. I had French toast loaded with powdered sugar, and I had to cut it up in tiny pieces and push it around my plate to make it look as if I was eating. Mom was happy. She had on jeans and a pink T-shirt and her hair was back in a ponytail again. I bet some people would think she was my sister instead of my mother.

"Kim, are you getting enough fresh air?"

"Sure, Mom, why?"

"You've got circles under your eyes. I want you outside more in the sun."

She was getting younger-looking from working, and I was turning into an old hag from all the worrying I was doing.

In the afternoon Willie and I sneaked over to Mrs. Mac's. Misty ran straight to us, and I noticed a collar around her neck.

"What's this?"

"Isn't that something? Remember I told you about my bingo friends, Mrs. Johnson and Mrs. Goldberg?"

I nodded.

"They work in a rummage shop on Sunday mornings, for the community center. And today someone brought in this perfectly good collar. And look." Mrs. Mac held up a black leather leash. "Now we can take Misty for a nice long walk and not be afraid she'll run away from us."

"Hey, that's great." Willie grabbed the leash and hooked it to the collar. "I want to walk her." He started toward the door.

"O.K., Willie. Just remember — don't walk to our house."

I washed out Misty's food bowl. Most of the time Mrs. Mac had everything done, and we just played with Misty. That wasn't fair. You couldn't have only the fun times, you had to share the bad times and the taking-care times.

"She's pretty well trained now, Kim. Whenever she wants to go, she scratches at the door."

I nodded.

"If my yard was fenced in, I could let her run out by herself. Now I tie her with a piece of clothesline so she doesn't get too far away from me."

My head would probably get loose if I kept

nodding. Our yard at home wasn't fenced in either. How was I ever going to bring Misty home? Even if Mom said O.K., who would take care of her? Now she knew every inch of Mrs. Mac's house. She'd probably be scared of ours and start to make trickles all over the place again.

Mrs. Mac put bowls out on the table.

"Are you cooking for someone today?"

"Yes, there's a young bride in one of the corner apartments. I'm going to make her five suppers for her freezer. Then when she comes home from work, she just has to warm and serve them."

"That's good. What are you making first?" She certainly kept on the go. Mrs. Mac never missed a chance to make some money.

"Meat loaf. And she has a couple of friends who may want some dinners, too." Mrs. Mac pointed to an empty mayonnaise jar with a slit in the cover. "This is for the tax money." She sighed. There were two dollars in the jar. She was sure going to have to cook a lot of meat loaves to save up three hundred dollars. I wished I could help. I thought of Mom and the PTA money. No, I had all I could do just to cover my own expenses.

Monday morning, Mrs. Brock spoke to me

during homeroom. "Don't forget, Kim. The other five dollars is due this week for disco dancing."

Oh, brother. Now *I* was going to get dunned by the PTA. Mom would surely remember that she had given me the money for this. I'd have to use my allowance and find some other money for Mrs. Mac.

Lisa passed me a note. "Have you seen E.F. this morning? Where are you going this afternoon? Is E.F. going with you?"

E.F.? I had to think to realize she meant Eddie Feeny. Before I could answer, I got another note from her. "E.F. and Doug are good friends. Maybe we could all go together!!"

Scott walked past my desk. "How's Eddie, Kim?" He snickered and a bunch of kids laughed. All morning long I was teased about Eddie. You would have thought we'd eloped instead of leaving the gym to visit my dog! Last year I used to play ball and stuff with boys without getting accused of all this love business.

In the cafeteria Eddie walked past me. "Hey, Eddie," somebody yelled, "you just passed your girlfriend."

"In your ear!" he yelled back. But he didn't

say hello to me, and his face was all red. He must have been getting teased all morning, too. I wonder if the PTA knew how silly their disco dancing was making kids act.

Willie and I planned Misty's bath for Wednesday. I found a big bottle of shampoo that hadn't been opened yet and a couple of old towels. They were still fluffy but had big holes in them. Mom had put them away for the beach, so I knew we could use them for Misty. I also took Daddy's hair blower to dry her quickly so she wouldn't catch a chill.

I couldn't make up my mind whether to tell Eddie or not. He didn't deserve it. Just because the kids teased, he stopped talking to me. As if it were my fault. Finally I decided to give him another chance. Some people are just weaker than others. I called Tuesday night.

"Hey, Eddie, this is Kim."

"Yeah. What do you want?"

"I just wanted to tell you that Willie and I are going to give Misty a bath tomorrow afternoon."

"Yeah. So?"

"Well, you said you wanted to know."

"O.K., so I know."

I slammed down the phone. That's what I

got for being nice! If he wanted to miss out on a lot of fun because of some creepy kids, that was all right with me.

Mrs. Mac had an old rubber wash basin on the linoleum. She even had paper spread around. No matter how early we got there, she was always one step ahead.

Misty's tail was wagging and she was all excited. "Ow!" Willie yelled as she jumped up to him. "Her nails scratched." You could see a red line on his arm. We'd have to cut her nails again. They had grown since the visit to Dr. Lyons.

She stood nice and still while I took off the collar. Her whiskers were twitching. It's funny the way the black and white are spread out across her body. Her ears, her forehead, and around the eyes are black. Then the rest of the face is white except for her black nose. Her back has one big patch of black and one smaller one. Even her tail is half black and half white.

I poured the shampoo into the basin and tested the water. Willie stirred it and made lots of bubbles.

"Maybe you two should put aprons on," said Mrs. Mac. "You'll be plenty wet otherwise."

"Not me," said Willie.

"I'll take one." I knew I'd have to do most of the scrubbing. "Here she goes." I picked Misty up and plopped her into the water. She wouldn't sit down. Her legs and back stiffened, and she tried to get out. "Quick, grab her, Willie."

Water was sloshing over the sides of the basin as we tried to make Misty sit. She wagged her tail, and soap and water splattered all over us. She tried to shake the water from the rest of her body. The soap was really making her slippery.

"Somebody's at the door." Mrs. Mac went to open it.

"Her head isn't wet," said Willie. We had her whole body wet except for her head. She still wouldn't sit down. I scooped up a handful of water and put it on the top of her head. Willie rubbed it in. She stood looking at us. The bubbles made a crown. Then she sneezed and sprayed us both. "Oh, it's in my eye." Willie stood up and was hopping on one foot. "My eye, my eye, where's a towel? Where's a towel?"

I couldn't let go of Misty. I held her with one hand and stretched to reach the towel that was thrown over the rocking chair. "Over here, Willie. Come over here." I grabbed it and tried to toss it. Misty took advantage of my loosened grip, jumped out of the basin, and ran across the floor. I let go of the towel and lunged after her, falling chest first into the basin, which tipped over onto the floor.

"Hey, what's going on here? This looks like a car wash." It was Eddie.

"Quick, grab Misty before she gets to the other room."

"My eye, my eye's still stinging. Make it stop, Kim." I stood up dripping. The apron hadn't helped. The water had soaked right through my T-shirt and was dripping down into my jeans. My sneakers were squishing from the water on the floor, and the ends of my hair were wet. I spit bubbles, wiped my face and arms, and then rubbed Willie's face real good.

Misty was in the corner shaking herself to dry off.

"Come on, Eddie," said Mrs. Mac, "off with your shoes."

"What a mess," he said, but he pulled off his sneaks and rolled up his jeans.

The floor looked like someone had spilled a can of paint over it. Water and bubbles were making trails across the checked linoleum.

"It was time to wash this old floor anyway." Mrs. Mac handed Eddie an old sponge mop. "You wipe up that water." She filled the sink with clean water. Willie was still crying. "Let me see that eye, Willie. Oh, it's fine. Just a little soap bubble. Go pick up Misty."

Misty ran across the wet floor and Willie slid after her. "Hey, I just wiped that," yelled Eddie. As they ran back across, I grabbed Misty and put her in the sink. We ran water over her, trying to get the soap off. But it was deep in her hair, and the more we washed, the more it lathered. After we had rinsed her with about two tons of water, it seemed to be out.

Now my jeans were soaked right through to my underpants and everything. "Let me dry her," said Eddie. He handed me the mop. "I didn't come here to wash floors."

He put Misty on a piece of newspaper and rubbed her dry. "Not too rough," I said, "she's only a pup."

"Oh, she can take it," said Eddie. "Let's plug in the hair blower." He blew Misty dry. Mrs. Mac gave Eddie an old hair brush. He fluffed her right up, and Willie snapped on the collar. "Boy, she really looks pretty."

"She really does." I was leaning on the mop.

"You look like a wet noodle, Kim." Eddie turned the hair blower on me full force.

"Hey, stop," I yelled as the hot air caught me right in the mouth. "It's my clothes that are wet." I pulled out my shirt and tried to help it dry by flapping it away from my body while Eddie aimed the blower on me. It took a while, and I was still pretty damp, but I could always tell Mom I'd walked under a lawn sprinkler.

"Refreshment time." Mrs. Mac brought out some cookies. I didn't feel bad about eating them, because I knew they were part of a batch she had baked for one of her working brides.

Before I knew it, Misty was curled up in Mrs. Mac's lap on the rocker. She was sound asleep, probably knocked out from all the excitement. I was sure glad we didn't have to do this every day. I bent down to kiss her ear. She smelled terrific. Well, the shampoo was supposed to make you smell like a garden in Hawaii. It had special conditioners in it and everything. I hoped she didn't smell too sweet. The last time I'd used this brand, I got attacked by a dozen mosquitoes the minute I stepped outside.

"Maybe I'll bring a bow for your hair tomorrow," I told her.

"Yuck," yelled Willie. "No bows."

"No bows," agreed Eddie. "Misty's a dog

to have fun with, not dress up like for a show."

We left a clean puppy, a clean kitchen floor, and a plate cleaned of cookies.

Eddie pointed away from the house. "I'm going to walk home this way, O.K.?"

"What for?" asked Willie. "We pass right by your house, Eddie."

"I have to go this way."

"We'll go with you."

"No, I have to stop and get something for my mother."

"Come on, Willie," I said, "I'll race you home." I guessed that Eddie didn't want any of the kids to see us together. I didn't care. After all, he *had* come to help with the bath.

"Hey, Kim, are you going to disco dancing again this Friday?"

"Yeah, I guess so, why?" I turned around to face Eddie.

"Well, no sense getting a new partner and getting all mixed up with the steps and everything. So why don't we stay partners?"

"O.K. with me, Eddie."

"See ya, Kim. So long, Willie."

"O.K., Willie," I said. "I'll give you a head start in the race. You start running, and I'll count to ten and follow you."

"Make it twenty."

"O.K., twenty. Get going. One, two, three . . ." I started to push the damp sleeve up off my arm. It felt funny. I rubbed my arm and looked down. The string bracelet wasn't there. I looked all around. I couldn't see it anyplace. That was funny. I was sure it was there this morning. Or was it? Maybe it had come off while we were bathing Misty. I hadn't even noticed. I had been so sure I would know the minute it fell off. I wondered if Lisa would say anything.

"Hey, Kim, look where I am already. Are you racing me or not?"

He was halfway down the block. That was nothing, I could still catch up and beat him with no sweat.

"You can't catch me. You can't catch me," Willie was yelling over his shoulder.

I slowed down to any easy jog and let him go. He looked so cute. And little kids get a kick out of winning things like races. I remember that Daddy always used to let me win. I could see why. Sometimes you could have more fun letting the other person think they won instead of winning yourself.

twelve

On Friday morning, Willie told us he was going over to a friend's house to play after school. Mom was delighted. She was giving us a ride because we were late.

"That's wonderful, Willie. Can you walk home by yourself, or should Kim come to get you?"

"No, it's just Peter's around the corner. I can walk home by myself." She was so happy you'd think he had just announced the climbing of Mt. Everest. It was really her fault that he never went anyplace alone. She was always busy being scared about his allergies. I was happy, too, except that today was Friday. I gave him a pinch. He jumped and I gave him a double-whammy look, which meant "Shut up, I'll talk to you later."

As soon as we were dropped off, I started yelling. "You've got some nerve. You know today is disco dancing. I have to go to that. Who's going to take care of Misty?"

He dug his sneaker in the dirt. "Peter asked me yesterday, and I want to play."

"Terrific. What am I supposed to do?"

"Can't you call Mrs. Mac and say we're not coming?"

"That wasn't the deal. We're supposed to be there every day after school to give her time off." I knew what he meant, though. It wasn't that I didn't adore Misty, but sometimes when I heard Lisa or the girls planning something, I wanted to go with them. It was a big responsibility hiding a puppy.

"Maybe we can skip going over there just this one Friday."

I called Mrs. Mac during lunch. She was nice. "Don't worry, Kim. Misty and I will be fine."

I felt worse when she hung up — maybe because she and Misty would be fine. They probably wouldn't even miss us. Misty had the yard and that nice rocker. She even had a nice soft lap to cuddle up in. Not to mention bingo on Tuesday. She'd be the only dog in

New Jersey, probably in the whole world, that went to bingo every week.

Maybe it was my mood, but disco dancing was horrible. Sure, I had a skirt on this week and so did the other girls, and everyone was real friendly. Mr. Chucka Chucka had on the same shirt as last week. Maybe it had his rhythm built right into it. Only this week, along with the gold chains around his neck, he had a whistle. He kept blowing it right in my ear. "All right. Let's line up. We're not going to waste time like we did last week."

Eddie was right next to me. "Gee, hope he goes over the steps from last week. I almost forgot them."

I remembered and started showing them to Eddie. The whistle blew again. Eddie grabbed his ears. "He's going to have blisters on his lips if he keeps that up."

"Or give us blisters of the eardrums."

The whistle again. "No. No. You can't have the same partners as last week. We have to learn to dance with all different partners."

People never leave well enough alone when they're teaching kids. Just when everybody had gotten over being silly about last week's partners, Mr. Chucka Chucka was going to turn it all around.

He made us count off by twos. I guess he

had been talking to the gym teacher. When we finished, I was partnered off with Doug, and Eddie was on the other side of the gym with Rosalie Rosenbaum.

The teacher turned on the music and started reviewing last week's steps. Doug wouldn't put his arms around me. "I don't touch girls," he said. He danced with his hands crossed behind his back.

"How are you going to do the hustle turns if you don't touch me?" I asked.

"I don't touch girls." And he looked over his shoulders to make sure the rest of his friends were watching. They were. Watching and giggling. As if by a signal, they followed Doug. They dropped the hands of the girls they were dancing with and crossed their own hands behind their backs.

Mr. Chucka Chucka stopped near us. "Now, you know that isn't right." He was sweating. I wondered how much the PTA was paying him and if it would pay for the nervous breakdown he would probably have when he was through with us. He took Doug's hands and forced one around my waist and the other to my hand. As soon as he passed us, Doug dropped them both. "I don't touch girls."

Oh, brother! Lisa was in love with this? On the other side of the gym Eddie was dancing with Rosalie, and they were doing all the turns and everything.

"I have to go to the girls' room," I said. "Just stand in the middle and tap your feet until I get back. You're really dancing by yourself anyway."

Lisa and Amy were in the girls' room. "Oh, you are the luckiest," said Lisa.

"Yeah," said Amy. "Last week Eddie and now this week Doug."

"Has he said anything about me?" asked Lisa.

"He hasn't said anything."

"Oh, come on. He knows you're my best friend, Kim. Did he tell you he likes me? Did he say where the boys were going after disco?"

"He didn't say anything except that he doesn't touch girls."

They both burst into hysterics. "Oh, I know," said Lisa, "isn't that a riot? They made up that they weren't going to touch their partners."

Maybe there's a special air bubble over my house that is keeping me from breathing the same atmosphere as my friends, because I never understand what they think is so funny. Maybe they don't understand me either, because Lisa said, "Oh, you're so serious this year, Kim. You can't even take a little joke."

"Yeah," said Amy, who was starting to bug me more than anybody, because she was like a mountain echo. Everything Lisa said, she repeated. Didn't she have a mind of her own? Or was she afraid to say anything original?

I suffered through the rest of the afternoon, but was I glad to go home! The whole lesson had been one big fat waste. And now I was out another five dollars and I still didn't know any more disco steps. Maybe the PTA should first have a course for the boys in touching girls to work them into this dancing stuff slowly.

When I got home, Mom was humming. The grill was on outside, and I could see pieces of chicken barbecuing. She must be in a good mood.

"Was your plan accepted?" I asked.

"Not officially, but it looks pretty good. I presented it at the staff meeting today, and the big bosses took copies to study. So I'm very hopeful."

Willie came rushing in. "I smell chicken. Here's a note for you from Miss Foster,

Mommy. I had a good time at Peter's." He was turning into a nonstop talker.

Mom was peeling fresh carrots. She gave us each one. "Eye power," she said as she opened the note. She looked right up. "Now, what's this all about? Aren't you drinking milk in school, Willie?"

I stopped chewing and spit the pieces of carrot into a napkin. If I choked on the carrot, it would make such a lump in the back of my throat that it would never go down.

Willie kept chewing. Mom read out loud: "Dear Mrs. Bowman: If Willie doesn't want to have milk anymore with the class, would he like to have some orange juice? It's the same price per week, a dollar and a half. Miss Foster."

"What's this all about? Why haven't you been getting milk every week, Willie? Where does the dollar and a half go to that I leave you every Friday?"

Willie stopped chewing. He looked at me.

Teachers sure kept track of things. I never thought that Miss Foster would notice that Willie wasn't buying milk. Or care. No wonder we couldn't grow up to be independent when parents and teachers were always checking on us.

Mom kept going. "But you always liked

milk in school, Willie. You drank it through kindergarten. Don't they still give you graham crackers with it? And you know you need it for your bones. And your teeth. Your TEETH!" She took the carrot away. "Open your mouth. Let me see your teeth."

Did she think they were going to turn black because he hadn't had milk in a few weeks? Besides, I had been pouring gallons into him at home to keep him healthy.

She went to the refrigerator and poured two glasses of milk. She pushed them both across to Willie. "Drink," she said.

Willie looked at the carrot on the table. "What about the carrot?" Mom hesitated. She was caught between his teeth and his eyes. I guess she decided that he needed his eyes to see the glass to drink the milk to make his teeth strong, because she told him to eat the carrot.

"I think Willie doesn't drink milk because it's white," I said. My hands were sweating.

"Then I'd like to know where the dollar and a half is that I've been leaving him here every Friday."

I was tempted to tell her that there was a puppy across town that had healthy eyes and teeth thanks to Willie's milk money. We used it every week for puppy food.

"Well, where's the dollar and a half been going?"

"For the milk," said Willie.

Mother pointed to the note. "But Miss Foster said you don't drink it."

"I don't, but I give my money to Peter, and he buys the milk."

"To *Peter*? Why to Peter?"

"Because . . ." Willie paused. I could almost see inside his head, and if there are wheels there like they show in the comic books, his were turning. I held my breath. "Because his mother gets Social Security, and they don't have enough money for milk."

"Social Security?"

My stomach sank. *It was a good try, Willie,* I thought.

"Willie, you have to be sixty-five years old to get Social Security. And I'm sure Peter's family can afford a dollar and a half for milk money every week."

He put down the carrot and lowered his head. Mom bent over and patted him. "All right, Willie, so you've been giving the money to some other kid because you didn't want to drink milk. But you should have told me. Miss Foster has a good idea. If you don't want milk, have orange juice in the morning. At least you'll get some extra vitamin C."

We were off the hook. Willie did better when he didn't talk. All he had to do was look miserable, and nobody could resist him. But that was the end of the dollar-and-a-half milk money. Now Willie would have to use it to buy orange juice. I'd have to find some way to get extra money for Misty's food. I wondered if they had a government health-care program for underprivileged puppies. We might be needing it soon.

thirteen

Lisa called early Saturday morning. "What are you doing today?"

I was still yawning, but I put my guard up. "Why?"

"I just thought we could spend the day together."

"What about Amy?"

"Oh, I'm sick of being with her."

I wondered if she ever said the same thing about me. "Well, what about Doug or Scott or the rest of the kids?"

"Honestly, Kim, just say yes or no. I don't have to get a whole third degree, you know. I thought we could go to the mall. My mom'll drive."

I hadn't been to the mall with Lisa all year. We used to have great times walking around and having a snack. It would be lots of fun. . . . But I hadn't been to see Misty yesterday. I absolutely had to go today. What was the matter with me? I wanted to go. It was just such a drag going back and forth. If she were only in the house all the time, I wouldn't have this problem.

"Lisa, maybe I can go this afternoon. But this morning I have to go you-know-where."

"O.K., I'll go with you. How is Misty anyway?"

"She's great."

We agreed to meet at eleven. Willie was going off to Peter's again, and I didn't stop him. After all, a little kid needs friends to play with. And he was really great about keeping his mouth shut.

Lisa met me and we went to Mrs. Mac's. Misty ran toward me as usual but stopped when she saw Lisa. She barked at her.

"Don't worry," said Mrs. Mac, "she's doing that because she doesn't recognize your smell, Lisa. You haven't been here for a while."

It took a few minutes of Misty sniffing around Lisa before she finally decided to accept her and stop barking. I snapped on the leash and we started out for a walk.

"Let me walk her," said Lisa.

"O.K." I handed her the leash. Misty was so cute. She had to stop and explore everything. Every blade of grass, the trees, houses. She'd stand perfectly still, ears up, until a car passed, then she'd take off and we'd have to run to keep after her. She'd slow down to watch a butterfly or a bird go by. At one of her stops I just had to reach down and give her a hug.

"Lisa, I don't want to go through Main Street. It's Saturday. We might meet someone who'll tell my mother."

"Don't be silly. Besides, I'm holding the dog, they'll think it's mine. And maybe we'll run into Doug or some of the kids."

Doug again. I had had enough of him yesterday, but I didn't want to spoil the day by telling that to Lisa. She must have planned this, because when we turned the corner, there were Doug, Scott, and Eddie. They were leaning on their bikes next to the drugstore. She handed me the leash so she could stop and fix her hair.

Eddie leaned down to Misty. "Hey, Misty. How are you doing there, girl? You still nice and clean from your bath?"

"What bath?" asked Lisa.

I looked at Eddie. His face got all red. Now he would have to admit that he had helped me bathe Misty, and all the teasing would start again. I helped him out. "I told Eddie that Misty had her first bath this week."

"Cute puppy," said Doug. "Whose is it?"

"It's Kim's," said Lisa. I didn't like this. Too many people were getting to know about Misty. It was bound to get back to Mom and Daddy some way.

"We're going riding. Want to go home and get your bikes?" asked Doug.

"I thought you didn't touch girls," I said.

"Well, I don't have to touch you when I'm on my bike."

"That sounds great," said Lisa. "We'd love to go." She used the same pinch on me that I give to Willie.

"What about the mall?" I asked.

"We can go to the mall any time."

"Yes or no. We're ready to leave." Doug was on his bike riding circles around us.

Misty was tired of standing in one place. She began to pull on her leash. "I don't want to go," I said.

"Just a minute. We have to have a small conference." Lisa pulled me over to the door-

the mall for the rest of the afternoon, and neither did I. We were having too much fun playing with Misty. We decided to try to build a dog house for her. Mrs. Mac had some old wooden crates and a couple of ripped-up quilts. We hammered and nailed away while Misty jumped in and out of everything. It was almost time to go when we finished lining the inside of the box with leftover scraps of material. It looked like an Arabian Nights tent, all draped and pleated. Misty crawled right in and curled up. I was sure she would have exotic dreams in such a fancy house.

Eddie stopped by on his way home from town and Lisa got giggly again. She stopped herself before I had to kick her. We showed him the dog house, and I nailed the top together while he and Lisa held each side.

Before we said good-bye to Mrs. Mac, I managed to get Misty alone in a corner of the kitchen and tell her not to worry, that I would be back tomorrow. I think she really understood me because she lay so quiet and peaceful in my arms. Still, whenever we left she always ran back to Mrs. Mac. She loved to climb into her soft lap for a quick snooze. I hoped she realized that I was her mother, not just some playmate that came around now and then. Mrs. Mac could be her grandmother. That was all right, because grand-mothers aren't really responsible for your life.

Lisa invited me to sleep over, and we stopped at my house to ask Mom. The answer was no. Mom and Daddy had a party to go to, and it was too late for them to get a baby-sitter for Willie. I was feeling sad because Lisa and I had had so much fun, and I didn't want it to end. Mom must have seen my face, because she said, "Tell you what. Extra money tonight for baby-sitting." Wow! That perked me up. Extra money. Maybe I could convince them to go out every Saturday night or Friday night or both. I would tell Mom she needed some rest and relaxation. I locked the door and put the chain latch on. Willie got the popcorn out.

We stayed up late. We popped corn about nine o'clock and then watched one of those thriller-chiller movies. Rather, I watched. Willie was in the room, but his head was un-der a blanket and a pillow was over his ears to block out the screams from the set. "I'll change the channel, Willie," I kept telling him. But he was asleep long before it was over. My eyes were shutting, too, and I dragged myself and Willie upstairs.

I think I heard Mom and Daddy come in.

I don't remember exactly, but I did feel the covers being pulled up around me and a light kiss on my cheek. That was Mom. She always checked us before she went to sleep.

I thought I heard ringing in my dream and someone calling "Kim, Kim." But it was so nice and snuggly in bed that I just burrowed myself under deeper.

Suddenly the lights went on and before I could get used to them, Daddy was shaking me. "Kim, come on, Kim, wake up. We need you downstairs. The police are here."

The police! Daddy looked very serious, like the day he had told Mom he couldn't afford to send us to summer camp this year.

"Put on a robe." A robe? I never wore a robe. I stumbled to the closet and found an old sweat shirt on the floor. Daddy pushed my hair out of my eyes and I followed him downstairs. Mom was talking to the policemen.

"Officer, this has to be a mistake. We don't know any Mrs. Macvey, and my daughter doesn't own a dog. It's impossible. She's in sixth grade at Deerfield School. My husband and I work all day. How could she get a dog without our knowing about it?"

Mrs. Mac . . . Misty . . . I shouldn't have watched chiller theater. I was probably having a nightmare. I didn't have time for any more thoughts. There were two big, tall policemen in our living room, and one of them was holding Misty. "Ouch," he yelled. He dropped her to the floor quickly and shook his finger where a tiny drop of blood was forming. She must have bitten him. She was barking and ran right under the coffee table, jumped over the lamp wire, and ended up at my feet. She pulled at my pajama leg with her sharp little teeth. I picked her up quickly. Her whole body was trembling, just like on the first day I got her. I hugged her close and petted her till the barking stopped. There was no way I could say I didn't know her. She shot out her tongue and covered me with big wet licks from my forehead to my chin. Mom and Daddy just stared at us. Finally the policeman who had been talking broke the silence. He opened his notebook. "Now, Mrs. Bowman, you were saying that the dog couldn't possibly be your daughter's?"

fourteen

The next hour was a blur. I do remember that Willie woke up and came down. "Hi, Misty," he said, and Misty ran over to give Willie a lick.

"You mean Willie's been in on this, too?" asked Mom. Willie didn't even seem surprised to see Misty in our house or realize that the jig was up. Maybe he was walking in his sleep. Daddy carried him back to bed, and he didn't complain.

"Answers," Mom said. "I want some answers." Before I told my story, the policeman told us that Mrs. Mac had taken ill in the night. Pains in her chest. I couldn't believe it. She had looked perfectly fine yesterday.

She had called her neighbor Mrs. Goldberg, who called the first-aid squad. Before she was taken to the hospital, she told the police about Misty and made them promise to bring her to my house.

"She kept talking about that dog. She wouldn't let us take it to the pound even though it was so late. Said that Kim would be scared to death if she came around to-morrow and found nobody home. Said some-one had to feed the dog. She also said," the policeman read from his notebook, "to tell Kim she was sorry she had to be the one to break the secret, but she was sure you and Willie wouldn't be mad at her."

"Will she die?" I asked. I thought people went off in ambulances when they were going to die.

"They think it's a heart attack."

"Doesn't she have family?" Mom asked.

The other policeman spoke up. "We called a daughter." He flipped open his book. "Charlene Miller, in Ohio."

It must be horrible to have a heart attack in the middle of the night. I hoped it wasn't because of her having to take care of Misty and my always bringing friends around, and all the cooking she had to do. She always seemed full of pep. And now Charlene would come out from Ohio and find out about the taxes and make things rough for her.

"We're waiting, Kim." Daddy's voice brought me back into the room. Misty was in my lap, and I thought she was asleep. Mom and Daddy and even the two policemen were staring at me, waiting. I just remembered that I hadn't gotten Misty a license yet. They might still take her to the pound!

I started to talk fast. About the animal shelter, Norman, the ad in the paper and the deal with Mrs. Mac, and the trip to the vet. Mom interrupted once. "So that's why you always needed money." I admitted about the milk money and the PTA money and the disco money. It almost felt good to be telling everything. I realized how uncomfortable I had been with all the stories I had made up.

The policemen left and Misty woke up. She began sniffing around the furniture to get acquainted.

"I think she has to go outside, Mom." Mom jumped.

"Well, quick, take her into the yard. That's all we need now is for her to make a mess in the house." I realized I didn't have her leash, but we had some old string in the kitchen, and I tied that to her collar.

It was dark out and chilly. I huddled underneath my shirt while Misty sniffed her new surroundings. "I don't mean to be nasty, Misty, but could you please hurry? My feet are freezing." She was taking her time. I looked up and saw a couple of stars twinkling, and for some reason that reminded me of Mrs. Mac. I shivered again, but this time I knew it wasn't from the cold. Misty finally found a spot in the grass to do her business, and I hurried her inside.

"I know you're mad, Mom, but could we please call the hospital and find out how Mrs. Mac is?" I looked at the floor. "It wasn't her fault."

Mom called and was told that Mrs. Mac was listed as critical.

Daddy put his hand on my shoulder. "That doesn't mean the worst, honey. Usually anyone brought in by ambulance is listed as critical."

Misty had curled up on the little mat in front of the kitchen sink. "Let's get back to the dog, Kim."

Daddy put his arm around Mom's shoulder. "You know what? It's very late and we've all had a big shock. I think everything can wait until morning."

"Maybe you're right. But what are we going to do with the dog?"

"Don't worry, Mom. I'll take her up to my room."

"You're not going to put her in your nice clean bed, I hope."

"She's clean. We gave her a bath the other day. You can even ask Eddie Feeny. He helped us."

"That's nice. Eddie Feeny was in on it, too. Who else?"

"No one. Honest. Well, I forgot Lisa. But she's my best friend. And maybe a couple of other kids from school know about it. Honest, that's all."

Daddy turned off the living room lights. "Tomorrow. Good night, Kim. Tomorrow we'll talk over everything."

I showed Misty all around my room. I was afraid she'd wake up suddenly and be scared. I shut my closet door so she wouldn't wander in by mistake. I also pushed the chair against the wall so she wouldn't bump into it.

I got under the covers and put her next to me. She curled up on the pillow, and her tail was wagging right in my face. I moved away a little bit and turned the light out. She barked. I think she was looking for me. "Shh," I said and moved closer.

I could feel her breathing on me. Her tail wagged more slowly, then it stopped. I patted her back. She didn't move. Her head was so soft, down between her ears, her little nose. She was asleep. I had dreamed about this so often. I didn't have to stand at the window tonight and say good night from a distance. But I hadn't expected it to happen like this. Mom's face had looked so angry. Her lips were all white and tight. Even Daddy, though he was trying to keep things peaceful, had been shocked when Misty ran to me. And Mrs. Mac . . . what if she had to stay in the hospital a long time? Who would water the plants in her house and earn money for the taxes?

When I woke up, there was sunshine in the room. I felt stiff. Then I remembered Misty. She was still curled up next to me. I had been lying on my side all night so I wouldn't disturb her. I got out of bed slowly and rubbed my shoulder. Misty opened her eyes the minute I moved. Her tail was wagging and she started to bark. "Shh, Misty." I picked her up. "It's me, Kim, remember?" I put her down and she ran around the room, sniffing, sniffing, nose into everything. I remembered what that meant and rushed her downstairs. I didn't want any accidents before Mom got to realize how lovable she was.

Mom was already in the kitchen making coffee. That was a bad sign. She was usually the last one up on Sunday. I ran out the door with Misty and waited while she sniffed all around the yard. Finally she found the place where she had gone last night and went. Mom watched from the doorway. I hoped Daddy would get down soon. Mom was hard to handle alone.

Willie bounced downstairs. "I had a dream last night . . ." He spotted Misty. "It's true. It's Misty. You really are here." Misty took off like a flash, and Willie rolled around and around the floor with her.

Sure, leave it to a little kid. He was just happy that Misty was here, didn't even ask how it happened. Mom was smiling at them. Well, they did look cute. Willie was nuzzling his head into her stomach, and Misty would lie stiff for a minute and then jump up and run around him and come back for more. Maybe that would melt Mom's heart. Willie sneezed. I held my breath. This was no time for allergies.

Daddy was yawning as he came into the room.

"Your father and I were up all last night . . ."

"Your Mother and I were talking . . ."

They had both started at once. Daddy stopped. "You first, Phyllis."

"Can I call the hospital and find out about Mrs. Mac?" Anything to put off the conversation.

"What about Mrs. Mac?" asked Willie. "What happened to her? How did Misty get here?"

"Speaking of that dog," said Mom, "isn't anyone going to feed her? Look at the time, it's practically noon." I knew Mom really had a soft heart. Otherwise it would be easy for her to get rid of Misty. She could just let her starve to death.

I dialed the hospital while Daddy and Willie fixed Misty some mushed-up bread in milk. We'd have to go out and buy dog food. Mom found an old bowl that didn't match any of our other dishes.

"Here, use this," she said.

The hospital still wouldn't say anything except that Mrs. Mac was critical. And only members of the immediate family were allowed to visit.

"Kim, sit down and we'll talk." Mom pulled my chair out. Misty finished eating and was sniffing around the room again.

"Mom, she's got to go out."

"Again? Is something wrong with her bladder?"

"No," said Willie. "She just ate, and puppies always go to the bathroom after they eat because eating starts their stomachs working and . . ."

"O.K., O.K., spare me the details." Mom put her hands on her head. "Take her out."

Willie had the door open in a flash.

"Have you noticed how different Willie has been lately?" Mom and I both looked at Daddy.

"What do you mean?" she asked.

"I mean before you started working, Phyllis, that kid couldn't button his shirt by himself. Now look. Not only does he take care of himself, but he's taking charge of a puppy, too."

I chimed in — anything to keep them away from the subject of Misty. "You should see him in school, Mom. He's not afraid of any of the big kids anymore. He has lots of friends. I can hardly keep up with him."

"Well, I'm glad he's become independent, but there are some people around here who are too independent. As a matter of fact, too big for their own britches, as we used to say."

Since we were through discussing Willie, I guess she meant me. The phone rang and Daddy went to answer it. After a few minutes he called me.

"It's for you, Kim. Charlene Miller, Mrs. Mac's daughter."

Mrs. Miller told me she had flown in from Ohio and gone straight to the hospital. Mrs. Mac had definitely had a heart attack but was resting comfortably. She'd have to be in the hospital a few weeks. Mrs. Miller also said that Mrs. Mac sent us her love and a special hug to Misty.

"Can I come by the house and pick up her leash and her dog food?" I asked.

"Sure, that's why I'm calling. Mother was worried about all of you. She said to remind you that Misty has to have another shot next week."

"I'll remember. And Mrs. Miller, would you please water the plants in the house? Especially the coleus? Mrs. Mac, I mean your mother, was just reviving it. She always watered it about four-thirty in the afternoon."

"You and my mother are some pair. She's in the hospital worrying about you and that dog, and you're home worrying about her and her plants."

"Are you going to stay in New Jersey?"

"Of course. I'm going to try to close up the house and get things organized. As soon as

Mother gets out of the hospital, she must come home with me to Ohio. This time she'll have to listen to reason. She's just too old and weak to live by herself. I'll just leave everything on the porch, and you can pick it up whenever you want to."

After hanging up the phone, I told everyone the news.

"But who'll take care of Misty?" Willie had come in on the tail end of my sentence.

"That's what I've been trying to discuss all morning." Mom slapped the table. The phone rang again. "Now who is it?" she said.

It was Lisa. "Do you want to come over?"

I told her I couldn't, but she wouldn't hang up. She wanted to know if I was going to Mrs. Mac's. Quickly I tried to tell her what happened. Mom was motioning me to hang up. Finally we were all seated around the table again.

"Now can we please discuss what we're going to do?" asked Mom.

"My coffee's cold," said Daddy.

She ignored him. "I couldn't sleep a wink, Kim. First of all, I couldn't understand how you could lie to us. And then all that maneuvering with the money. Why, that was like stealing."

Daddy interrupted. "Well, not exactly stealing. I'm sure Kim was intending to pay it back."

The back of my throat was all stuck. "I wouldn't steal, Mom. Honest. I was going to pay it back. If you had let me go to my bank account, I could have kept up with the expenses."

"Can Misty sleep with me tonight?" asked Willie.

"No, she sleeps with me," I said.

"Just a minute." Mom slapped the table again. "Who said she was going to sleep with anyone? As a matter of fact, who said she was going to stay in this house?"

There was a little squeal from the corner. Misty had spilled some water from her bowl onto the floor and was trying to lap it up with her little pink tongue.

"I think she heard you, Phyllis," said Daddy.

I was getting nervous. I had always thought there would be plenty of time to prepare Mom for a puppy. This might be too much of a shock for her.

We just kept talking and talking, and all our words were making a gigantic spider web, with Misty caught right in the middle.

Finally Daddy said, "This is silly. We're going to waste what's left of a beautiful Sunday."

Mom stood up. "You'd better work out a schedule for taking care of that dog. Then we'll have to decide on a punishment for you, Kim. And your baby-sitting money will all have to go to repaying your debts."

"Then we can keep Misty?" asked Willie. I was starting to breathe again. I didn't care if they didn't pay me for the next fifty years. I'd gladly skip disco lessons, wear old clothes, and start my own plant-watering business if I could keep her.

"Not so fast, young man," said Daddy. "You were in on this little secret, too."

"Who, me?" said Willie with innocent eyes.

"Yes, you," they both answered. Daddy continued, "I think a little readjustment of your spending money should be in order, too, Willie."

It was decided. Misty would stay with us for the time being. There was no one else available. It sounded like Charlene was determined to take Mrs. Mac home to Ohio. Mom carried the cups to the sink. She didn't think anyone was watching, but I saw her pat Misty's head and tickle her behind the ears before she shooed her out of the way.

fifteen

The next couple of weeks went so smoothly I couldn't believe it. Our schedule worked great. Willie took turns with me feeding and walking Misty in the morning. I appreciated that. I love to curl up for an extra five minutes' sleep.

I came home at noontime every day. Lisa joined me. She would bring her lunch sandwich and eat it at my house after we fed and played with Misty. It was a private time for us to be together. It was almost like last year. I knew all her secrets, even the stupid ones about boys, and she knew most of mine.

Willie and I came home right after school to take Misty out, even if we had to go someplace. We were lucky, she hardly had any accidents. Well, one or two, but we were always able to clean them up before Mom came home.

We had one bad time when Misty found an old leather slipper of Daddy's and chewed it half up. That wouldn't have been terrible, except it made her throw up in corners all over the house. Mom sent me and Willie around with a bucket filled with detergent and ammonia to mop up. I had to carry another empty bucket around with us because it smelled so bad I was sure I'd throw up myself.

One night at dinner, I saw Mom slip Misty a piece of meat off her plate — something we were absolutely forbidden to do, so I knew she was really getting close to her. I began to feel as if we'd always had a puppy in the family.

The only thing I felt guilty about was Mrs. Mac. She was still in the hospital. I wasn't allowed to go because they don't allow visitors under sixteen. Mom and Daddy went to visit her one night. They brought a big geranium plant.

I sent along a letter in which I told her how Misty was behaving. I told her about the second rabies shot and how Willie and I were taking turns sleeping with her. I also told her I thought Misty missed her a lot. Many times she would stop dead still in the house and look around as if she wasn't sure where she was. Willie drew Mrs. Mac a picture with colored pencils and wrote a nice get-well message on the back.

Eddie Feeny stopped by practically every day to play with Misty, too. Once he brought his poodle along, but the dog was so scared of Misty that he started shaking, and Eddie had to carry him around until he calmed down. "Boy," he said, "I wish my mother would let me get a dog like Misty. This poodle is only good for showing off. He's so nervous you can't have any fun with him."

Some days it was annoying to have to run right home after school to take Misty out — especially if everyone was going someplace. Having a dog was a full-time responsibility, just like Mom and Daddy had said. But Mom was up for a promotion as a full personnel manager because of her vacation plan, and I didn't want to give her anything to worry about at home.

Charlene, Mrs. Mac's daughter, called us one night. "Mother's coming out of the hospital tomorrow." It had been four and a half weeks. I was glad she was coming out, but nervous, too. What if Mrs. Mac wanted to go back to our old routine of having Misty stay with her? I didn't have to worry.

"I've settled up everything," continued Charlene. "My husband drove out, and we are taking Mother right home with us. The hospital has sent her medical records to my doctor in Ohio, and they all agree she can make the trip. We're going to drive nice and slow."

Poor Mrs. Mac. I thought of her little house. Sure, it was run-down, but it was all hers. She could do whatever she wanted to in it. Even though her garden had lots of weeds and overgrown grass, she still grew some nice flowers and vegetables. And what about all the pots and pans she used for her cooking business? And the big rocker that she used to sit in with Misty? And the lamp that tilted to one side? I doubted that her daughter would let her take all that stuff. And what about the weekly bingo? Did they have bingo in Ohio? Even so, it wouldn't be the same. She wouldn't have her bingo partners to play with.

"Kim?"

"Yes, Mrs. Miller."

"Could you and Willie and your mother and father come over on Saturday morning about ten? We're going to leave then. I know Mother wants to say good-bye to you. And could you bring Misty to say good-bye? Mother's going to miss her, too."

I told Mom and Daddy, and they agreed that we should all go over. Friday night Willie and I scrubbed Misty so that Mrs. Mac would see what good care we took of her. First we washed her with this special flea-free shampoo that the vet had given us. It was supposed to keep fleas away, but it smelled so bad it could keep everyone away, not just fleas. So then we washed her with Mom's special shampoo. It smelled like lilies of the valley. We brushed and brushed until her white parts were sparkling and her black spots were dark and gleaming.

Lisa came over when we were almost through. "Can I go with you tomorrow to say good-bye to Mrs. Mac, Kim?"

"Sure, Lisa." She could always surprise me. She was acting real sentimental about Mrs. Mac's leaving. Lisa gave Misty a big hug. "You smell delicious. All the little boy dogs are just going to be chasing you around and around and around."

"Boy dogs only chase girl dogs at certain times," said Willie.

"Why, Willie, you're so smart. But don't you think you're too little to be talking about the birds and the bees?" Lisa pinched his cheek.

"Ouch," he said, "don't do that. And I'm not talking about birds and bees, I'm talking about dogs."

It was time to change the subject. "Sure, you can go with us, Lisa."

Misty ran downstairs and curled up at the chair where Daddy was reading the newspaper. He would hold the paper with one hand and tickle her under the chin with the other. She just loved it. If he stopped, she'd nudge his hand and arm with her nose until he would begin again.

"Hmm, Misty, you smell just like Mom," Daddy said.

"I heard that," said Mom. She was going over some papers.

"Well, it's true. Misty, go over to Mom and let her smell you."

Mom sniffed. "My shampoo! Kim!" she yelled out. "Willie! Do you know how much that stuff costs?"

"Oh, Mom, it's a special occasion," Willie said.

"Special occasion or not. The cost of that shampoo comes out of your spending money, too."

If this kept up, I'd be paying back forever, and my children would probably have to continue to pay after I died.

We got to Mrs. Mac's at ten minutes of ten the next morning. It was quiet. The lawn was twice as overgrown as it had been, and the house looked as if one big huff and puff would blow it down.

Misty jumped out of the car, sniffed around the yard for a few minutes, and went right to the front door. She scratched and scratched on it. All the time she was yelping and making little whining noises. I guess she really had missed Mrs. Mac. All the smells were bringing back the good times to her.

Charlene opened the door. I hadn't realized it on the phone, but she was old. Mrs. Mac was so old that she had an old lady as a daughter.

Mrs. Mac was sitting in the kitchen in a wheelchair. No plants were around. I guess Charlene had given them all back to the owners. Lisa and Willie stopped still and stared. I couldn't blame them. Mrs. Mac was all shrunken up. In the past few weeks, her heart attack had pressed her in half. She had a blanket tucked all around her legs. Misty went crazy. She ran to the wheelchair and jumped around and around, pulling on the blanket, waiting to be picked up.

Mrs. Mac had only half the voice she did before she went into the hospital. "Hello, everyone. Oh, Kim, would you pick Misty up? I can't bend over yet."

I picked Misty up and handed her to Mrs. Mac. Misty licked her face, her cheeks, and her nose. Mrs. Mac talked softly to her and buried her face in Misty's ear. Misty curled up and kind of sighed while Mrs. Mac petted all around her head, under her chin, and the back of her neck.

Charlene petted her, too. "You were right, Mother," she said. "She is a pretty little pup."

There was a funny kind of lump in the back of my throat, and when I looked over at Mrs. Mac, I saw that she had tears running down her cheeks even though she wasn't making any sounds.

Everybody felt it. Charlene cleared her throat. "Well, we've got to be going now, Mother." She turned to us. "My husband's in the car already. We were just waiting to say good-bye to you folks."

"What about the bingo ladies?" I asked. Mrs. Mac still couldn't talk.

"They were here last night and we had some coffee and cake," said Charlene. She handed me a slip of paper. "Here's our address in Ohio. If you could drop us a line once in a while, I'm sure Mother would appreciate it. She'll be resting and sitting outside in the garden getting some sun."

Mrs. Mac still hadn't said anything. Just because she was sick and old, she had turned into the daughter and Charlene was acting like the mother, taking charge and making all the plans. I bet Charlene wouldn't let her dig around in that Ohio garden wearing old fatigue pants like she did in her garden here.

Daddy helped push Mrs. Mac outside. Misty was still snuggled up in her lap. There was a station wagon in the driveway packed to the brim. Charlene's husband was behind the wheel. I saw the old lampshade with the hanging tassels in the back and the red geranium Mom and Daddy had given her. I guess Mrs. Mac wanted to take some stuff from her old home. "Better give Misty back now," said Charlene.

Mrs. Mac handed Misty back to me. Daddy and Charlene's husband helped her into the back seat of the car and folded up the wheelchair. "Now, Kim," said Mrs. Mac, "you take good care of Misty. You, too, Willie. And Lisa, don't bug Kim when she has to take care of Misty. The boys will wait."

"I won't." Lisa got all red. Misty was quiet. I petted the back of her head. She couldn't know that she would never see Mrs. Mac again. After all, Ohio was pretty far from New Jersey, and unless we went on the automobile trip to California that Daddy had been promising us for years, I doubted if we'd ever go there.

"And take her for her checkups. She's a good dog, Kim." Mrs. Mac looked right at me. "You love her and she'll always love you. She'll never leave you all alone." I saw her look over at the house. "I hope the new people who come here don't cut down the rose bushes. If they just weed them out, they'll bloom real good this summer. And I was going to plant tomatoes in the corner." She pointed to the side of the house. "Could have sold them this summer, too. Last year I sold every cucumber I could grow. Bet the tomatoes would have helped me pay off the taxes . . ."

"Now, now," said Charlene. "We've been through all that, Mother." I didn't say a word. But the lump in my throat got bigger. Daddy had told me that Charlene had sold the house to builders. They were going to bulldoze everything down and build a store.

There wouldn't be any roses coming up next summer. But they didn't want Mrs. Mac to know. It would upset her too much.

Mr. Miller started the engine. "One more hug. Willie, come here." Mrs. Mac hugged Willie, then Lisa. She shook hands with Daddy, and Mom kissed her on the forehead. It was my turn. I couldn't stand it. She looked so little and sad and was leaving all her friends and everything she was familiar with. I leaned over and she put her arms around me and kissed me. Misty was squashed between us. "Good-bye, Kim. Please write and take some pictures for me."

"Mrs. Miller?"

"Yes, Kim." Charlene looked back over her shoulder.

"Did you say you had a fenced-in yard in Ohio?"

"Yes. It's a big yard, but we put up a metal fence so people wouldn't use it as a crosswalk."

"Then if you had a dog, Mrs. Mac, I mean your mother, wouldn't have to chase it because the dog couldn't get out."

"Well, no. The fence would keep the dog in. As a matter of fact, we had a pup a few years ago. But we don't have one now."

"Yes, you do." I put Misty in Mrs. Mac's

lap. Her hands closed around Misty's body. "Why, Kim," she said. "What's this about?"

"It's just that you're going to be home every day, Mrs. Mac. With a nice big grassy yard and fresh air. And I have to be in school every day. And we'll be having disco dancing two times a week pretty soon. I don't want to have to run home every day to take care of Misty." I linked arms with Lisa. "And in the spring Lisa and I are going to try out for cheerleading, and that'll mean practice every day. It's just too much responsibility for me." I spoke quickly, and I didn't look at Misty's big wet eyes. I wanted to snatch her out of Mrs. Mac's lap and run and run until everyone was gone and Misty and I were all alone. But I didn't.

Mom came and put her arm around my shoulder. She spoke softly. "Kim, are you sure you want to do this?" Leave it to Mom to understand. She wasn't personnel manager of the Denninger Company for nothing.

"But Kim," said Lisa, "we're almost through with disco dancing for the season."

I squeezed her arm against my side to warn her to keep quiet. Willie couldn't figure out what was going on.

Mrs. Mac grabbed my hand. "I shouldn't let you do this, Kim." She took a big breath.

Don't, I thought to myself. *Don't let me do it.* The tears were rolling down her cheeks again. "But this little dog'll help me from missing all of this . . ." She pointed to the house. Her voice sounded stronger. "I'll write you and send you pictures. Let's get going, Charlene, since we have to go all the way to Ohio. Misty and I want to see our new home. And I'm telling you right now: Misty eats only first-class dog food. None of those bargain things you always get at the supermarket. And if your church has bingo, Misty and I might just try our luck."

"Are you sure, Kim?" Charlene asked.

"Oh, I'm sure." Why didn't they just go? "You're really doing me a favor. I'm much too busy to take care of her anymore."

We all waved and said good-bye. They rolled down the driveway. Daddy came and stood on the other side of me. He kissed my forehead. "I'm proud of you, Kim. That was a wonderful thing to do." Misty was licking at the closed window. I wasn't proud of me. I was already sorry. I didn't think it was a wonderful thing to do. I thought I was a big jerk.

"Hey." Willie just realized what happened. "You gave away Misty. Kim gave away Misty." He started to cry and stamp his feet.

"Let's go," Mom said. "How about if we all stop for ice cream?"

"At ten o'clock in the morning?" asked Willie through his tears.

"Sure," said Mom, "why not?"

"I'm going to walk home. I don't want any ice cream," I said.

"O.K., Kim," said Daddy. "And maybe when you get home we can have a talk about puppies." I held my hand up for him to stop. I didn't want him to say that they were going to go out and buy another dog for me. I didn't want another dog. I wanted Misty.

They pulled out from the curb. I started home. I wondered if Misty would get car-sick on such a long trip. Well, she wasn't my responsibility anymore. Would she ever think of me and wonder why I wasn't around anymore? I didn't realize I was crying until I felt drops trickling down my cheeks. Someone ran up behind me.

"I didn't feel like having any ice cream either." Lisa put her arm around me. "I was thinking, Kim. Those string bracelets we did last summer were dumb. They don't last long enough. How about if we buy silver friendship rings? I saw some real neat ones in the five-and-ten."

The drops were plopping on the front of

my shirt, and my nose was running. I wiped it with the back of my hand, a slobby thing that I always yell at Willie for doing.

"How much are they?" I asked. While we were talking, Misty was getting farther and farther away from me.

"About six dollars. We could save up from our allowance."

I laughed through my snuffles. "Yeah, I'll have enough in the year two thousand and two."

"We'll think of a way. Our class trip money has to be in next week. Maybe we could borrow ahead on that and pay it back bit by bit.

"Yeah. Maybe." I wondered if they were on the turnpike yet. I hoped they'd stop every once in a while and let Misty stretch her legs. "You know, Lisa, I don't think we need strings or friendship rings to prove we're friends."

"Maybe you're right. They also had tiny neck chains with little hearts on them."

"Come on, I'll race you home." Maybe tomorrow I'd be happy that I had done such a nice thing for Mrs. Mac. I started to run.

"Oh, Kim," Lisa yelled after me. "I just did my hair this morning. What if we meet one of the boys? It'll be all messed up from running."